THE
SOCIOPATH

A Novel
by
J. V. Adams

JACKRABBIT BOOKS
Box 1
Minneapolis, Minnesota
55440 U.S.A.

"HARD TO BEAT"

DEDICATION

To the old gang from 54th and Lyndale, 'way back there in the 'Forties:

DuWayne Breault, Calvin Ells, Ralph Smith, Shorty Clouse, Curly Hill, Merrill Madsen, Adrian Huyck, Rollie Anderson, Gen Gangelhoff, Dick Gangelhoff, Kenny Allen, Jimmy Allen, Jim Daly, Franny Nielsen, Don Nielsen, Billy Nielsen, Clay Carter, Pam Pamplin, Maridean O'Brien, Juanita Crosby (Effie Tucker), Adele Hill, Terry Sarazin, Dick Roedel, Bert VanDerBerg, Harry Starring, Marty Christensen, Dick Smith, Stan Brown, Jimmy Cook, Clyde Cornelious, Pat McNally . . . and all those other good old kids from long ago and far away . . .

—"Nig"

--PERSONALTY AND BEHAVIOR
Copyright 1963 by Jesse E. Gordon, Ph.D.
University of Michigan
(Macmillan)

But before leaving the sociopathic personality, a few remarks about social attitudes
toward this kind of personality are in order.
Because of his lack of apparent anxiety and
the readiness of the sociopath to violate social
norms in order to gratify his drives and wishes,
the sociopath arouses strong feelings in other
people.   They respond either with intense
anger and resentment, or they idolize and
idealize him, making him a hero of folklore,
such as Bluebeard, Morgan the pirate, Jesse
James, and others.   These reactions occur
because the sociopath does what most of us
would like to do but cannot because of the
inhibitions

---

and conflicts that we have but he lacks. Thus
we admire him and keep him in our fantasy as
a folk hero, and at the same time reduce our
own guilt and control our own drives by trying

to eliminate him and his arousing effect on us from our environment. These reactions are complicated by the fact that the sociopath often is a charming and socially graceful person, again because he lacks inhibitions and anxieties cued off by other people. He thus seems both more admirable and more dangerous to our own self-control. In effect the sociopath is so much of what we would like to be and fear to be.

A further complication arises because the sociopath's relative freedom from interpersonal anxiety and from desires to conform to social norms provides some of the conditions for original and creative activity. Thus some creative sociopaths become literary and artistic heroes, and criminals in general are sometimes perceived as symbols of the creative artist rebelling against the constraints of a philistine society. Some novelists owe at least part of their fame to the public's response to their sociopathic personalities and to their colorful histories of having committed violence and defied convention. Similarly, there are many fictional heroes who serve as symbols of the free (and criminal) spirit. People often have a feeling of awe before a really flamboyant criminal, a feeling that he has somehow transcended to a new and ideal dimension the confines of our humdrum world. He has had experiences that go beyond our (conscious) imaginations—experiences that touch our own repressed drives sufficiently to attract us and to mix our rejection of his behavior with an odd attraction, a combination that produces our feeling of awe.

We recognize the relationship between creativity and asocial or antisocial behavior, and the extent to which we will tolerate the latter as the price of the former represents a real problem for our ideas about justice and the social good. This is one of the meanings of Dostoevski's Raskolnikov, who asks if a superior person can violate social prohibitions against murder. Thus far we have not found an enduring solution to this problem.

* * *

The man whose name I've been using for the past twenty-seven years actually died just south of Yongdung-Po, Korea, in the winter of 1951. The two of us were out on patrol alone that bleak November evening when I paused to take a piss and I was a good eighty yards behind him when he stepped on the mine. It tore off both his legs, his right arm, and his face. It also killed his ass on the spot.

When I got to him it was like I was playing a part in an old, familiar play. I took off his dogtags and exchanged them for mine. I pulled off his six-dollar Timex and put my hundred and eighty dollar Longines with the alligator strap on his one remaining wrist and I even switched his Camels and Zippo for my Pall Malls and engraved Ronson Whirlwind. And of course I gave him my billfold too and took his.

Then, as careful as could be, I removed his moneybelt and the one hundred and twenty-three thousand dollars in Won, Yen, script, and American greenbacks it held. And even as I was buckling this belt around my own waist I knew that in the days ahead I was going to lead a very colorful and exciting life.

No two ways about it, I definitely was one clever son-of-bitch. Within a month of hitting Korea I had found the biggest black-marketeer of them all and I stalked him and I set him up and I got him. It was no accident that I transferred TDY from the Air Force into his combat infantry Army outfit, it wasn't chance that put us out there alone on patrol that vicious winter night, and it damn sure wasn't just by luck that he circled the rocks to the right. He went that way because I told him to. I told him I had reconnoitered this area. And I had. I'd looked it over real good that morning when I planted the mine.

So now I was the boss. Now I had the money. Now I knew for sure that I was a genius of a schemer and the sky was the limit. From now on I could kill any man I wanted, I could overpower any woman I desired, and no one on this earth could do anything about it. Because once every three generations fate selects one lucky devil out of the billions for the ride to the very top and now I knew that I was the one.

And so it was, in this stinking rice paddy halfway across the world those many long short years ago that I realized nothing could ever stop me now because I was a child of destiny.

* * *

Promptly at nine o'clock the warden got on the intercom and said, "Are they out there?"

Eighty feet down the hall executive secretary Greta Keogh made neat little rows of circles on her pad and spoke without raising her eyes to look through the sound proof plexiglass separating her from the small waiting room. "Patman, Good, and Janski are here, Mr. Koch; Savanna is due in a moment."

"God dammit, I said I wanted this thing at nine sharp; what the hell's the holdup?"

"It was a mix-up on his clean khakis, sir," Miss Keogh said levelly, "They gave him someone else's clothes by mistake. He's through with his shower and Custody phoned at 0857 saying he would be up here not more than three minutes late."

"Son of a bitch; this is the sort of crap I can't stand." Paul Koch released the intercom switch, leaned back in his chair and pulled out a cigarette. Taking a deep drag, he stood up slowly and there was no trace of peevishness in his voice when he again spoke into the intercom. "Greta," he said, "come in here for a minute, please."

It was two minutes after nine when she closed the door behind her and was alone with the warden in his office. "Sir, I'm sorry this has upset you . . ."

No, no, no, it's OK. It's nothing. It's just that I don't relish giving these assholes the opportunity to bask in the slightest possibility that I am reduced to playing games. In other words, when I say nine o' clock I goddamn sure don't mean three minutes after nine, and they know it. Christ! they're the most sophisticated prisoners in the entire state. They might only wear those cheap commissary watches but they set them by the headphones and, believe you me, they know what time it is."

Greta Keogh sat down in one of the four black leather chairs arranged casually before the big desk and folded her arms. "It's no big deal," she said slowly. "They know they're one short and they won't start feeling smug until you keep them waiting after he gets here."

The warden was silent for a moment. "Look, Greta," he said finally, "When the Commissioner was over here Tuesday we got into the brandy and made a big dent." He hesitated.

"Now it's true," he continued slowly; "it's true that I initially planned to speak briefly with the four of them and then I intended to call them back one by one and lay it on the line on an individual basis."

"I know, Paul," Greta said.

"But, hell, this is OK. I'll just switch tracks. Like you say, it's no big deal anyway. As a matter of fact, this whole project stinks to high heaven as far as I'm concerned. These ding-a-ling sociologists have been the bane of us professional penologists for many, many years but now that they've got hold of this big Federal grant money the whole structure is being threatened and, by God, I hope I'm six feet under when these long-haired jerks finally learn the difference between idealism and reality."

A clear tone sounded twice and Greta stood up at once. "That would be Mary; Savanna is here."

"Fine! Send in Mr. Patman." The warden smiled, sat down at his desk, and lit another cigarette.

Greta stopped by the door. "What was it about the brandy?"

"Never mind," said the warden. "Have Larry run over to my house and bring back a cold case of Pabst Blue Ribbon."

Larry was a trustee.

"You bet," said Greta. And smiling, she walked back down the hall.

* * *

Vincent Savanna was alone in the shower room. Alone except for O'Neill, the guard.

"Come on, V. O.," O'Neill shouted out over the soft roar of the water, "For Christ's sake you've been in there long enough." He twisted the cold water faucet to OFF and instantly the room began to fill with steam as superheated water hissed from all seventy-two shower heads.

Savanna danced out into the aisle with a yelp. "You dumb micky shitass. Knock it off. Turn that cold water back on. At least give me a chance to rinse off the soap."

"OK, but you got exactly one minute left. The warden is waiting for you and, by God, my job is to get you there on time." O'Neill turned the cold water faucet back to its former position and Savanna went back into the shower stall.

Now, in the time remaining, Vincent O. Savanna, convicted armed robber, concentrated on the odd situation he had found himself thrust into less than thirty minutes earlier. Mentally he calculated the many possibilities. To be pulled off the job in the twine factory only an hour after beginning work; to be escorted by a guard to the shower room; to be told nothing except that the warden wanted to see him; what did it all mean?

Certainly it was no infraction of the rules that was behind all this. In the fifteen months he had been in prison following his being sentenced to 10-80 years for armed robbery, he had been careful to walk softly and keep a low profile while he checked out the legal remedies which quite often had meant a new trial, and sometimes even an immediate release, for a number of his fellow inmates. Then too, it was the Custody Office that dealt with punishable activity--not the warden.

And why the shower? Did he have a visitor? But again, the warden did not directly involve himself in anything so mundane as a visitor seeing an inmate. No, this obviously was an event of some special importance and Savanna felt a sense of apprehension and curiosity as he stepped from the shower, dried himself, and dressed in the set of fresh, newly pressed khakis which the guard had had him pick up at the laundry on the way from the twine factory.

The two men walked down the long main corridor of the prison and waited at the first of the four huge steel gates which barred the way to the front entrance. A guard in back of the gate, upon seeing them, immediately produced a large key, opened the gate for them, and then locked it behind them. This gate guard, who had no means of opening the second gate, called out to a guard seated at a control console two doors ahead.

Seeing O'Neill and Savanna standing in the first trap, this guard pressed the sequence of buttons which unlocked the second gate, locked it behind the two men after they entered the second trap, and then unlocked the third gate, admitting the guard and prisoner to the third and last trap where he himself was seated.

To the left of this small enclosure was a small waiting room where Savanna now expected to be taken for whatever business it was that the warden had with him. With a sense of incredulity he saw a guard seated at the metal-detection unit, just inside the glass, unbarred front door which led from the lobby to the street, rise, walk quickly toward them, and unlock the fourth and final gate.

Savanna thought, My God! we're actually out of the prison. And it was true. They were in a lobby not unlike that of any office building. A pop machine stood by the main desk, a number of vending machines lined one wall, and several laughing, chattering young women, one carrying four cups of coffee, clicked past. Pedestrians and traffic were clearly visible on the street just yards away.

"You're a little late," the lobby guard said to O'Neill, "I think he's waiting for you." He pointed to the left and O'Neill and the convict Savanna, walking faster now, headed for the office of Warden Paul Koch.

The door to the office was open and before O'Neill had a chance to rap an announcement of their arrival the warden looked up from his desk. "Come in, come in." He pointed to one of four black leather-upholstered chairs which were arranged in a semi-circle before him.

"Savanna, you sit down here; O'Neill, you can go back to your regular duties. We won't be needing you." The warden flicked a lever on the intercom: "Send in those three men, Miss Keogh; Savanna is here. They brought him in from the front."

The inmate tentatively unbuttoned the flap of his shirt pocket. "Go ahead and smoke," the warden told him. It might help you. Because I'll tell you right now you're about to get a real shock."

The three convicts who had been waiting down the hall now filed into the office. They walked somewhat stiffly, their faces showing puzzlement and concern.

"Please be seated, gentlemen," the warden told them, waving them toward the chairs, "and smoke if you wish. This really isn't going to take very long." He came around to the front of his desk, sat on it, and began talking.

"All the fine details of what's happening to you men today will be explained to you later by other people. I'm just going to give you a rough outline. In fact, I honestly don't even know a lot of the details. A certain number of us here in administration have been kept aware of developments in this particular program from time to time but the final authorization for its immediate implementation came through only last evening and so, as I say, there is a whole lot about it that I don't know myself.

"But the gist of the whole thing is that you four men are to be released from prison. Today. Right now. Well, within an hour anyway. The cars will pick you up at ten o'clock."

"What cars, Warden," Patman asked. "Where are we going?"

The warden paused a moment before continuing. "The four of you, as well as an unspecified number of other inmates from around the country, have been selected by the Department of Justice in Washington to take part in an experiment. I understand they used a computer. Naturally, our State Department of Corrections worked in conjunction with these people.

"Please understand that none of you are being released from your sentences; you are only serving those sentences outside of prison walls, much as someone on parole does." The warden picked up a paper from his desk and studied it briefly.

"Janski," he said, "you are going to be assigned to the Stearns County Veterans Hospital as a group therapy leader.

"Good," you are going to a half-way house up in Duluth.

"Savanna, you have been put on the field staff of the Department of Corrections.

"And you, Patman," he said, looking at the one black inmate, "you are going to be scheduled onto a speaking circuit designed by a group of lay people at St. Thomas College.

"And that's about all I can tell you people at this time," the warden said. "Cars will be here very shortly to pick you up and all of you are to return to your cells now and pick up whatever stuff you want to take out with you. Don't spend a whole lot of time doing this. Come back to the front gate as soon as you're packed up and the guard will admit you to the interior waiting room. As the people arrive to pick you up you'll be called out and from that point on you're under their authority and as far as I'm concerned you take orders from them. You'll be under their jurisdiction and I'm sure they can answer your questions far better than I. Does everything seem clear enough," the warden asked.

The four inmates nodded frozen faces and, rising, the warden opened the door to the corridor and dismissed them. "Fine. And the best of luck to each of you men; I sincerely mean that."

As soon as they had filed out he went swiftly to the phone and carefully dialed an eleven-digit number in a distant city. "John?" he said, when the phone was answered, "Paul, here. So far so good. Stunned? You bet they were!

"Great! Sure thing. You bet! I'll be in touch, John." Hanging up, Paul Koch took a can of Pabst from the small refrigerator built into his desk and a curious smile crossed his face as he popped the tab and took a long swallow.

* * *

None of the four inmates spoke as one by one each of the four gates was opened and shut for them. It was only a short distance from the last gate to where the two main cell blocks winged off the main corridor. Now Calvin Janski, alcoholic forger, and Aaron Good, bunko artist, turned left and headed for their cells in "A" House.

Oliver K. Patman, who had twice been acquitted of murder charges and who now was doing five years for negligent manslaughter, continued down the main corridor to "D" House.

Savanna turned right, entered "B" House, and climbed the metal steps to the third galley. Halfway down the block-long catwalk, when he was nearly to his cell, the solitary guard on duty down on the main level spotted him and called up: "Hey, Savanna, you're going out, eh!" Apparently the guard had been notified.

Vincent leaned over the railing and, reaching for a cigarette, lit it and talked down to the guard. "Yeah, that's what they tell me."

The guard, a young Viet Nam vet considered an 'OK Cat' by most of the inmates, wanted details. "What the hell, man; I thought you just got three years at the Board!"

"I did," Savanna replied, blowing a cloud of smoke, "but this is some sort of Federal deal; an experiment. I'm going to be working in the field for the Department of Corrections."

"I'll be damned! You're going to miss that twine factory, I'll bet!"

Savanna laughed and turned into his open cell. "I'll bet I don't, old buddy!"

Emptying his cell was an easy task. Unlike many convicts, he had never been one to accumulate. He set his small box of letters on the bunk, riffed through them briefly, and decided to discard them all. With this decision made the others were easy. Pictures, clippings, his pens--everything was thrown in the trash box with his letters. His several library books he placed on the bars of his cell, his earphones and bedding he put under one arm and, picking up the box of discards, he walked out of the cell without looking back and listened to the hollow sound of his footsteps as he walked firmly, and very alone, the length of the catwalk, down the steps, and up to the desk near the cellhouse entrance.

"That didn't take you long," the guard said lightly.

"No, I didn't have much stuff to go through. Say! where do you want this bedding? Should I take it down to the laundry?"

"Just throw it on the floor there," the guard said, "I'll have one of the galley-hops pick it up. I'll take your earphones."

Savanna walked to a fifty-gallon trash container and dropped in his box of possessions which only an hour ago had seemed so valuable. Now all he had was a small paper sack of toilet articles. "This shaving stuff I can use," he told the guard; "to hell with everything else."

"I got a pass here for you to go down to the tailor shop, Savanna," said the guard. "Get your suit, I guess." The man handed over the pass and made no attempt to hide his curiosity. "I don't get it, guy; what's this thing all about anyway?"

"Just like I told you. It's some kind of experiment. They've got a Federal grant and I was picked by a computer."

Several galley-hops had wandered down to the desk and they stood there with their brooms and dust rags, listening. "I heard Patman got picked too," one of them said.

"There's four of us," Savanna told him. "We're all going into different programs."

"Who are the other two?"

"Janski and Good."

"Aaron Good? That jew bastard is always pulling off some kind of deal."

"I sure didn't pull off any deal," Savanna said. "Shit, I was out working in the twine factory an hour ago. They just called me out and sent me up to the warden's office and they gave us all the news at the same time. As a matter of fact, I've been working on a writ of corum nobis. This is just a bolt from the blue to me and I'm pretty damn sure that the same goes for all four of us."

"Well, good luck to you," said the guard, sticking out his hand. "And stay away from this place."

"Thanks. I will."

Savanna shook hands with the guard and then with the two cellhouse workers. "Have a piece for me," one of them said, grinning.

"You bet I will," Savanna said, and a little burst of laughter echoed in the big empty steel and concrete cellblock.

* * *

The suit wasn't too bad, Vince decided, studying himself in the mirror. He had picked a brown gabardine from the long rack, and a pair of dark brown shoes. The suit fit. So did the light tan topcoat.

The two convicts who worked in the tailor shop had been watching him knot his tie. One of them said: "Most of the guys going out, I have to tie their tie for them; they've forgotten how to do it."

Vince had heard this before and he knew it was true. "I haven't been here that long," he said; "I've only been here fifteen months."

"Somebody told me you were doing ten-to-eighty."

"I was," Vincent told him, "but I fell into a special deal." He explained the situation to the two men and one of them whistled softly in amazement.

Leaving the tailor shop, Vince smiled as he thought of the little shock wave of excitement which would sweep through the prison as the news spread. And he knew it had already started. The prison grapevine was incredibly fast. Within ten minutes every man in the joint would know what had happened.

* * *

None of the other three men had arrived when Vincent entered the waiting room. He sat down and lit a smoke. Almost immediately a guard appeared. "Where's Good," he asked; "the guy's out here to pick him up."

"All three of them must be down in the

tailor shop," Savanna told him, "I'm the only one here."

"Well, the guy is waiting." The guard went away.

Now Patman showed up. He had been laughing at some joke with the gate guard and came into the room with a big grin. "Say, man," he said, "you sharp as a muther. How you like my threads!"

"Yeah, you're OK, Patman. What's in the sack, your lunch?"

Before Patman could answer the gate opened and Janski and Good came through together. A guard at the front desk spotted Good and yelled at him: "Let's go, Good; the man's up here waiting for you." Without ever entering the waiting room, Good walked up to and through the front gate and was gone.

The three men looked at each other. "I'm finally starting to believe all this," Janski said. Vince felt his palms getting damp.

Within minutes the front gate opened again. "Savanna," the guard called out. "Let's go; snap it up." Vince shook hands quickly with Patman and Janski. "Hang loose, you guys."

"See ya, Vince, baby!"

"Yeah; Don't come back!"

A thin young man, hardly more than twenty-two, was leaning on the front desk. "Hi, Savanna," he said, holding out his hand. "I'm Martin Fox. I'm going to drive you down to the Cities."

"Glad to meet you," Vincent said; "I'm ready to roll."

The guard at the desk spoke up. "Better take your money along; you might need it." He shoved a receipt out to be signed and Vincent counted out the $86.50 which had accumulated in his account.

"OK," Fox said, when the receipt was signed; "let's go."

Outside in the crisp and sunny November morning, Vincent looked around for some sort of staff car; something he expected to be a plain four-door sedan with lettering on the side. Following Fox, who bounded down the front steps two at a time, he saw the man instead open the door of a powder blue convertible parked at the curb, its top down and motor running. Astonished, and with the first tiny alarm now sounding far back in his brain, Vincent got in and fastened his seat belt.

The car was a new 450SL Mercedes with California plates.

* * *

"Are you a parole agent," Vince asked carefully. The sporty little car was humming down Highway 36 toward Minneapolis.

Martin Fox laughed. "Hell, no. I'm still in school. Engineering. U. of M. I'm sort of an errand boy as far as picking you up goes.

I've got some good friends in Corrections and I happened to be over there this morning.

"The parole officer you'll be dealing with won't be back in town until late this afternoon and so they asked me if I'd pick you up." Fox looked at Vincent and chuckled. "I suppose this is all quite a shock to you, eh!"

"Yes," Vince said slowly, "you could say that. I mean, what the hell, less than two hours ago I was running my spinners in the twine factory and now I'm in a new suit heading down the road in a brand new Mercedes-Benz."

"It'll all start making sense to you in a short time," Fox said. "All the pieces will fall into place."

"Where are we headed right now?"

"I'm supposed to drop you off at the Sheraton-Ritz Hotel. They've paid for your room for one night, until you get a place lined up, and I'm supposed to tell you to be in the Cheshire Cheese at seven-thirty tonight. Your p.o., George Gannon, will meet you there at seven-thirty sharp."

"They? Who's 'they'?"

"The Department of Corrections, who else. That's who got you out and that's who you'll be working with."

Martin Fox had more to say. "As far as drinking goes, they said to tell you they don't care about a couple of beers, but don't overdo it because this Mr. Gannon has something important to tell you and you're not to be bombed out of your head.

"Your folks live here, don't they," Fox went on. "Why don't you go visit your old man, or go to a movie or something, to help you kill time."

"Oh, I won't have any trouble on that score," Savanna said.

"The main thing is to remember that they want you there in the Cheshire Cheese on time. It's a restaurant on the second floor of the Sheraton. You'll see it."

When they got to the hotel, Fox merely pulled up to the curb and waited for Vincent to get out. "The room is in your name," he said. "And lots of luck to you!"

Baffled, apprehensive, disbelieving, Vincent slammed the door shut. "Thanks," he said weakly. Then he stood watching as Martin Fox, with a smile and a wave and a little squeal of rubber, melted off into the noontime traffic.

* * *

With the shade down and the curtains drawn the room was still dark. But the instant I opened my eyes I knew it was morning. I could tell by the sound of the traffic outside and by the way I felt.

What a strange little hotel this was. It was only about one block from Grand Central

Station and I always stayed here when I was in N.Y.C. The rooms rented for $4.00 per night, plus tax, and there were only eleven of them, all on the second floor of a grimy old building.

I got out of bed and put up the shade and stood there awhile looking down at the dirty cars and the fast-walking people in the street just one story below. Then I put on my pants and, taking my billfold, I went out into the hall and locked my door and walked down to the shower room.

It was pretty quiet; no one else seemed to be up yet. As I showered I thought about this small hotel with a sort of pensiveness. Years earlier I had found it by asking a newspaper vendor if he knew of a cheap, clean place and this was where he had sent me. It had been a good tip. Indeed it was clean. The blankets were old and threadbare but they smelled vaguely of soap and the walls and hall were clean too and the ashtray was washed daily and even the bathroom, if old and worn, was well-scrubbed and pleasant smelling.

How could anyone make a living renting out only eleven $4.00 rooms, I wondered. Once I had seen a maid picking up sheets and at least two different people worked shifts in the cashier's cage and so at least three people made a living on $44.00 per day, less taxes and overhead. This was less than I'd once earned in eight hours of only leaning on a broom in a California aircraft plant--and I considered myself vastly under-paid.

Such a world! What a difference there was in people and what it took to make them happy. One man's snack is another man's feast.

I had never been locked into one frame of values or ideas. All the roads of my mind stretched on out to infinity. None of them went in circles and there were no fences. Anything seemed possible and nothing seemed even remotely improbable. This very day I might be eating lunch at the White House with the President of the United States or tonight I might be dancing and sharing a joke with Miss New York City herself!

One thing I was very sure about how-ever, was that I never wanted to get one of my legs chopped off. Once I had broken a leg and for six months I'd had to limp around on crutches. I remember feeling frustrated but also quite impressed at how quickly my all-valuable mobility had been restricted. I'd never dreamed how precious this mobility was to me nor had I even vaguely realized how I took it for granted. Without a bit of hesitation or a moment of doubt I decided that if I ever had a choice of losing an arm or a leg I would absolutely give up an arm. No one really needs two arms but, sweet Jesus! I do indeed need my two legs. They are what move me from here to there and time after time I'd found it extremely urgent to get out of here—and not on crutches, but fast!

The traffic was louder and the sky was brighter when I finished shaving, went back to my room, and dressed. Maybe it was about seven o'clock. I'd accidently left my watch on a bar in Las Vegas three months earlier and had never bought another. Deep in my heart I did not like watches or clocks of any kind. I found them mildly disturbing. I really did not care what time it was anyway and with clocks all over the world it had never seemed any problem getting along without one of my own.

I was dressed now, not really warm enough for February in New York, but I could always pick up a sweater or a heavier jacket later on. Maybe my heavy boots and flannel lumberjack shirt would stamp me a hayseed in Manhattan but, hell, since when did I give a rat's ass about other people's opinion of me. It was my opinion of myself that counted, no one else's.

Even knowing I'd probably be on a plane leaving New York this afternoon, I paid the desk clerk for one more night because you never know what might come up and these rooms were always rented by 5:00 P.M.

Out on the street I ambled along with my hands in my pockets, soaking up with great interest all the sights, sounds, and smells. I'd never been in another city where human beings dug through the trash barrels for half-eaten wiener buns, split-covered bagels, candy bar wrappers and whatever else could be crammed in their mouth, with animal grunts, to be washed down with dregs of pop cans and the melted ice in the paper cups of the fast-food chains. All this in broad daylight without a trace of self-consciousness and in full view of throngs of uncaring, well-fed New Yorkers.

An amusing idea sprouted in my brain. How would it be if I bought a couple dozen hot dogs, sprinkled them with cyanide, rewrapped them carefully, and tossed them one to a trash basket all along Lexington about five o'clock in the morning, just before the animals went looking for breakfast. Wouldn't God be pleased that I had cleaned up the city a little bit; wouldn't there be less piss and vomit in the doorways of New York if twenty-four of these depraved pigs were removed! Certainly there would always be those who would start screeching at the "immorality" of it but, shit! it's results that count and no one could deny that my little contribution had helped a little.

I went into an Italian deli, sat at the counter, and ordered a cup of black coffee.

"Cream and sugar?" asked the waitress.

I was used to this. "Black is fine," I told the stupid broad and gave her my most ingratiating grin.

* * *

Half an hour later I got off the elevator on the forty-eighth floor of the Chemical Bank Building and walked into John Vanderberg's office. Plainly, the receptionist was not impressed by my appearance. "Did you have an appointment?" she asked coolly.

"He's my brother," I said. "Tell him Chris is here; I'm just passing through and I'd like to say hello."

Instantly she turned friendly. "Just go right in, Chris; he'll be glad to see you." I knew in my heart that John wasn't going to be all that tickled to see me again and when I was seated across the desk from him I could see I was right.

"Chris, dammit, I thought you said it'd be next Monday you'd be here."

"I did, but I know how fast and efficient you are, John, so I came a little early."

John's tone combined mild exasperation and pride. "Well, Chris, this time you happen to be right. It's all taken care of. There's a few loose ends to be tied up, a couple phone calls and maybe a memo or two, but the tricky stuff has been done and you got what you wanted."

I sat there for a while and let this soak in. Finally I said: "Was it hard to pull off?"

"Anything's easy if you know how to do it," John answered. "In this case it took a bit of maneuvering, let me tell you."

35

"You always were pretty foxy, John."

"I'm shit compared to you, Chris, and we both know it.

I lit a smoke and looked at John curiously. "How did you do it--or shouldn't I ask!"

"Hell, that's all right. I had a team of guys from L. A. draw up a proposal and we submitted it to C.E.T.A. through regular channels. Of course I had a few wheels greased before it ever got to Washington and I included a feasibility study which was very impressive."

"Was it fake?"

"No, not really, but it was definitely slanted. I don't know if those people could see through it; I don't know if they even cared. Anyway, the whole damn package was approved."

"Who were these people who actually wrote the proposal?"

"It's a group of hotdogs in Long Beach, California. They do all the C.E.T.A. proposals for Southern California. Well, not all of them, but a least a big percentage. They specialize in getting funds for blacks and chicanos and they guarantee their product or there's no charge."

"They sound like a pretty smart bunch."

"Damn right. They'll deliver an M.A. thesis in a week, three weeks for a Ph.D and, for Christ's sake, they'll even do an application essay for a kid shooting for admission to an Ivy League college!"

I thought to myself, damn! what's this country coming to anyway. Aren't there any decent people left.

John continued: "The touchiest part of the whole deal was getting the Dept. of Justice to go along with it. Alvin Burke was responsible for getting us the formal nod."

"You mean that guy took money, a retired general!"

"No, we made a quid pro quo deal. He's been screwing around with grain futures in the midwest and I'm letting him hook into our big IBM computer here until he recoups his losses and maybe gets a couple bucks ahead."

"Jesus, man, that's flat-out stealing," I said.

John laughed. "No more so than using a WATS line for a personal call. The bill is the same every month whether you make ten calls or ten thousand."

"No chance of you getting burnt?"

"None whatsoever. I'm in charge of this baby and I told Burke it was only time I could give him; the software end of it was his own problem."

My mouth was a little dry. "Have you got a beer, John?"

"Yes, I do," he replied, "but I'm not giving you anything to drink. You told me more than once that every time you got in trouble it was when you were drinking."

I sat there half annoyed, half amused, and studied John carefully. Nearly fifty now, he was graying and slightly paunchy. A bigshot with IBM, I marvelled. Sixty, maybe seventy thousand a year while I'm out there scratching and scrambling for it. Life had been easy for John—well, it had been easy for me too, but only because I used my wits; nobody ever gave me anything.

"OK, skip it," I said; "just tell me what happens next."

"The guy you want happened to be doing a robbery sentence in Minnesota State Prison. Actually we ran over two hundred thousand cards through and we found five that were really great but this guy turned out to be our best bet."

"How's that."

"Well, one's on death row in Alabama, one is seriously ill, and the other two have been released and we don't know where they are— they just disappeared."

"Tell me about this guy, John."

"I haven't got the make-sheet right here; it's at home. But he's a smart bastard, I can tell you that. He doesn't have the highest I.Q. in the prison but his psychological profile indicates he is almost insidiously clever. He can think five different directions at the same time."

"Has he been released?"

"He gets out tomorrow. Actually, there are four getting out but that's just to make it look good. Over the next month or so we'll nail the other three for something or other and have them returned to custody."

Now John leaned across the desk and spoke very intently.

"Chris, I've done the best I could for you in this matter and, dammit, I don't intend to keep sticking my neck out. I'm not pissed off at you or anything like that but I want you to leave me out of any more of these schemes you dream up and I hope you understand me clearly when I say I'm done now, finished, kaput, <u>out</u>. In other words, anything you ask me from now on, the answer is 'no'!"

"How about Korea, John."

"All right, how about it! Korea was a long time ago, Chris. Those days are done. From now on you can paddle your own canoe. OK?"

I sat there thinking. "You say this guy's getting out tomorrow? Where will he go?"

"Somebody will drive him over to Minneapolis and line him up for a meet."

I snubbed out my cigarette and was about to go when a new thought struck me. "Say!" I said suddenly, "are there any funds connected with this deal?"

John laughed. "There probably could have been," he said, "but no, the proposal specifically stated that the project was to be independently financed. That might have had something to do with its being approved. Why, do you need money?"

"That'll be the day," I snorted.

"Are you going to Minneapolis to talk to this guy, Chris?"

"Which reminds me," I replied, "you never told me his name."

"His name is Vincent O. Savanna."

"No, I'm not going to Minneapolis," I said; "I've got better things to do. Besides, what would I want to talk to a punk like that for."

After I left John's office I picked up my suitcase at the hotel, caught a cab to the East Side Station, and took a Carey bus to JFK. I got off at the TWA terminal, paid cash for a ticket, and by twelve noon I was halfway to L.A.

* * *

God, I was sick of planes. They weren't the same as they used to be. The food looked good, I'll say that much for it, but it tasted like crap; like it was made by a machine. And most of it was, I suppose.

And what a scuzzy bunch of stewardesses they had these days. I thought back to 1958, when the commercial jets first came out, and I remembered how fresh and pretty

and really beautiful all the stews used to be—
not at all like those sloppy, worn out, droopy-
breasted skags you found working the skies
nowadays. Delta was the worst offender, I
thought. Jesus! that line had bitches in
uniform that should have been put out to
pasture before Camelot faded. Thank E.R.A.
for that, probably. The airlines couldn't get
rid of the long-tooth sluts for love nor money.
Till death do us part!

Say! now there's an idea. Someone
ought to organize an "Old Stews Convention,"
pack 'em in an old beat-up DC-10 just before a
major overhaul was scheduled, and fly the
whole bifocalled, varicose-veined herd off to
the Canary Islands. Halfway there a person
could arrange to have a wing or two come off
and, shit! that's the end of about four hundred
problems!

Bet your ass! That's what's called
T.C.B. I smiled with satisfaction as I tilted
back my seat, shut my eyes, and listened to
the steady drone of the engines. In just a few
hours I'd be landing at LAX. Nancy would be
at work of course, but I had a key. I'd go out
there and shower and maybe have a scotch and
milk and when she got home she'd only have to
take one look at my face to know I'd pulled it
off.

"That's right, Nancy, babe," I'd say;
"Everything so far has gone just perfect. And
now, by God, we're going to have a little

action!"

* * *

In the seventy-seventh year of his life, Cecil Cohen realized that all of his troubles were due to the simple fact that he had lived too long. There was satisfaction in being a survivor, hell! he could die tomorrow and they'd have to admit he was one of the last leaves on the tree—but it was the passing away of the world he'd always known that he found hardest to bear.

Death itself had long ceased to be a dramatic event, no more important than a sudden summer shower, a passing freight train, or a farm dog howling in the night.

Melo's death left him hollow and vaguely angry but after all their long married years together he'd known it would and had expected, anticipated, something far worse. He remembered looking down at her face as she lay in her coffin and thinking, 'Well, now she knows.' And leaving the graveyard, especially with the other people around, he was conscious of feeling once again, utterly and finally alone. It's very true, he thought, that we're born alone, we live largely alone, and we're damn sure going to die alone.

Here in his two-room trailer forty miles west of Minneapolis he spent his days reading and thinking. Sometimes he would watch TV on one of the two channels he could pick up from the Cities but there wasn't much on the tube that interested him and even the books he picked up here and there weren't as good as they used to be.

His eighty acres were rented out to the Erickson brothers now and that plus his social security check meant there was nothing he wanted that cost money that he didn't have. But who would ever have guessed back there in the 'Thirties and the 'Forties that there were days like these to be endured. He wondered if others found change as painful, as embarrassing, as he did.

There was no reward, no recognition, no honor nor respect for all the learning and suffering it took a person to stay alive and grow old. Worse, one saw, unmistakably and regularly, that distain and mockery were what he got from the young. The painful part of it was that deep in his heart he couldn't blame them. All his knowledge was obsolete, all his stories sounded stupid, even to himself, and even his old moral code and rules of conduct seemed corny and full of holes.

"Ain't nobody on earth can fix a carburetor on a '36 Ford like old Ceece Cohen!" He remembered how proud he used to feel—back during the war—when people used to say this, and know it was true, and respect him for it.

What the hell! did I actually believe

that I was going to be looked up to for the rest of my life just for this? Did I really think that schoolchildren were going to assemble in reverent awe before me as I year after year explained the correct jet size and gasket thickness and all the other unimportant things to remember about 1936 Ford carburetors?

And, dear God, who wants to listen to the story of a fellow who worked sixteen hours a day, seven days a week, and laid five thousand dollars cash, in hundred dollar bills, mind you, five thousand dollars cold cash on the table and bought his own eighty acre farm before he was thirty years old! What was this supposed to be, this story—some kind of a lesson on the value of hard work and thrift? The last time he told it was to that snotty-nosed Bianchi punk who had replied: "Shit, man, that freak must've been stupid. My brother makes more bread than that in a month just dealing a little dope around the schools."

* * *

After he was arrested, Cecil Cohen tried to answer the detectives as honestly as he could.

Q.   "Why did you move out of your house in the first place, Cecil?"

A.   "Because I didn't want to live there alone. After Melo, Camille,—that's my

44

wife--after she died it was too big and empty for me. The trailer suited me fine. I'd set it up out there by the pond so the kids would have a place to warm up when they'd ice skate and it was a cozy little place. Had electricity, a hot plate, a refrigerator ... no running water but I used to fill up a two gallon ..."

Q.   "All right, never mind about that. So then you rented out the house to Zeff and Eckman?"

A.   "Not Eckman; he showed up later. I let Zeff live there for three or four months and I think he was supposed to pay me fifty bucks a month but he never did."

Q.   "You let a complete stranger live rent-free in a four-bedroom house?"

A.   "I liked the guy. He didn't really have any money anyway and I felt better with somebody there. Lights going on and off, smoke coming out of the chimney . . . you know what I mean. Besides, I believe in the corporal works of mercy: Feed the Hungry, Give Drink to the Thirsty . . ."

Q.   "He always had money for beer and cigarettes; didn't that strike you as a little strange?"

A.   "I honestly DO believe in the corporal works of mercy, gentlemen. To me it's not what a guy preaches that counts but what he actually does. Ever since I was a kid I ..."

Q.   "Fine, Cecil. But you did know

that he was never broke."

    A.   "He built that chicken coop on the west side of the pond. He used to sell about eight dozen eggs every day to the 7-11; used to bring some down to me too--all I wanted."

    Q.   "It took money to bring that D-4 Cat in when they started digging. Did you think that machine was being rented with egg money?"

    A.   "That was after Eckman turned up. I figure that he probably . . ."

    Q.   "All right. We'll get into that later. Tell us how you met Zeff."

    A.   "He just blew into town one day and I used to see him hanging around the bowling alley and the pizza place and sometimes down at the oil depot--the co-op-- and one day he sat down next to me at the municipal bar and asked me if I'd rent him my trailer. Said he'd been sleeping in a wrecked school bus out at the salvage yard."

    Q.   "But instead, you moved into the trailer and let him have the house. Why?"

    A.   "I liked the guy. You could talk to him two minutes and know he was no dummy. He had lots of interesting stories to tell--things he'd done, places he'd been . . . besides, like I said, I was tired of banging around in the house and it cost me a fortune to heat the place. Zeff, he picked up a wood stove and ͡ aled off all but the one room--the

46

kitchen—and he stayed there. Brought down a bunk from upstairs, and some blankets . . ."

Q. "What did those guys do all day, Zeff and Eckman?"

A. "Seems to me they just sat there at the table and talked. 'Course, I wasn't up there that often—every other day maybe."

Q. "How about women. They have any visitors?'

A. "I saw a blue car up there once or twice—a real expensive car, a convertible— but, no, I can't say I ever saw any women or girls."

Q. "Any chance they might have been wired?"

A. "How's that?"

Q. "Wired. Geared. Gay."

A. "Oh, shit no. They were no queers."

Q. "How do you know?"

A. "I can spot a queer a mile away. No, whatever else those guys were they weren't freaks."

Q. "How about booze. Did you ever see them drinking?"

A. "Zeff had a beer the day I met him down at the Municipal, but I don't think they ever drank at the house."

Q. "You never saw any whiskey bottles or beer cans?"

A. "As a matter of fact they had two cans of beer on a shelf by the window and, hell, a couple months later they were still sitting there—full cans. That's how I know those guys never drank; guess they just didn't care for the stuff."

Q. "OK. Now, how about after they rented that Caterpillar. Did you know what they were doing?"

A. "Indeed I did not. They said a contractor friend of theirs needed a place to store it for awhile and they had given the man permission, figuring I wouldn't mind--which I didn't."

Q. "And you never actually saw them doing any excavating with that Cat?"

A. No. That was in March and a couple days after the machine showed up I took off for California. I always go stay with my sister in Whittier for a month or so toward the end of winter."

Q. "Did Zeff know this--that you used to leave every March?"

A. "I don't know. I guess maybe I might have mentioned it."

Q. "Did you or did you not mention it."

A. "Yes, it seems to me I did."

* * *

"We'd like to thank you for your cooperation, Mr. Cohen."

"Never mind all that business. How

about getting me out of jail."

"That's not up to us."

"How about getting me a reduction in bail then. I mean, my God, fifty thousand dollars!"

"That's up to the county attorney. But I wouldn't be surprised if he recommended you be released on your own recognizance."

"He ought to. Hell, I haven't done anything. I just got caught up in this thing by pure accident."

"We don't know that. And until we get to the bottom of it we're going to be asking a lot of people a whole lot of questions."

"It's still a crappy deal to lock up an old man like me with all these drunks and perverts and trashy bastards."

"We're just doing a job, Cecil. And when you do get out don't be going on any long trips because we're certainly going to want to talk to you again in the very near future."

* * *

The young deputy sheriff would have driven Cecil Cohen all the way back to the trailer but Cecil said, no, just drop me at the edge of town. I want everybody to see that the big famous gangster is out of the slammer. It isn't every day these hayseeds get to lay eyes on a real, genuine criminal like me; give the sons-of-bitches something to talk about

49

besides their goddam rheumatism."

The deputy was one of Ivan Klein's nephews or grandsons or something, Cecil couldn't remember which. "Oh, come on now, Mr. Cohen, nobody's calling you a gangster."

"I'm still going to get me a good stiff drink. Besides, I have to stop down at the paper. They're bound to want a statement from me–a new picture too, probably."

Later, nursing his rye and lime rickey at the Municipal bar, Cecil felt a wave of melancholy sweep over him. He was stiff from the three days he had spent on the hard bunk in the county jail and there was no one here at the bar to talk to except Tina the barkeep, and she was too young and thick to understand or care.

Once this place had been filled with the sound of familiar voices. But they were all gone now--Emil, Big John, Ivan, Lucy, Maude-- Cecil stared at his drink. Gone, all gone. Mary and Rosie, Joey McKay, The Kraut, even Father Tom and Lucky . . . Yes! this place once had boomed and rattled with shouts and jibes mixed with the sound of the old Hank Williams records on the juke.

"Another drink, Mr. Cohen," Tina asked.

"I'll tell you something, kid," Cecil told her; "the thing about this world is that you never know at any one minute which of the people around you are going to be an important part of your life twenty years from now. A man might think that the answer would be real obvious. Like he'd probably say his wife, his kids, his brother, or his pal. But it usually doesn't work that way. Like, how old are you, Tina?"

"I'm twenty-four, sir."

"What would you think if I said that twenty years from now the most important people in your life might be that ten-year-old boy who delivers your paper, or a girl making donuts in south Omaha this very minute, or a Negro lad born in Chicago last Sunday morning."

"I don't think that's very likely."

"Like hell it's not. That's the way it goes. I'm just trying to tell you that you never know how much to invest in anybody else because you never know how long they'll be a part of your life.

"One thing I can damn sure tell you," Cecil continued, "and that is to never make your happiness dependent upon another person. Because it doesn't work."

Tina wasn't interested; she began polishing glasses. "You sound like a regular philosopher, Mr. Cohen."

"We're all philosophers," Cecil said moodily. He'd known this nitwit was too stupid to pay attention. He was going to stop coming in this place unless he could find someone to hold an intelligent conversation with. And he wasn't going to go over to the newspaper either. He didn't want his picture taken any more. He was fed up with this town and everybody in it.

He took a gulp from his drink and felt a knot in his stomach as the thought of the two detectives and all their questions rose up in his mind. He knew he had not told them the whole story and maybe that was wrong. Maybe everything is over now, he told himself. But then again, maybe it isn't. Maybe a whole lot more people are going to die unless I tell them.

Troubled, vaguely disturbed, he set down his half-finished drink and buttoned his coat. The two-mile hike to the trailer was just what he needed. He wanted to think.

* * *

When Nancy Rausch was a child she used to pass a cookie factory on her way to school. Right next to it was a huge pit where the factory used to dump its garbage and this pit was crawling with rats. On bright and sunny days these rats were never visible. Only when the sun went down, or on dark and cloudy days, did they emerge in hordes to boldly and unblinkingly go about their ferocious activity. Sometimes, returning home after dark, she would run past the dump in horror. But there were other times when she would deliberately stop and watch them, returning their fearless stares and enjoying the heavy pounding of her heart.

These days it was something else that emerged after sundown. Her painful brooding; her seething hatred. During the week, at least through the day, things weren't bad. The simple mechanics of living occupied enough of Nancy's time and energy to relegate the evilness to an abscure recess of her mind. But sooner or later the evening would come. Evening was the worst part of the day and Sunday evening the worst of all.

Her work week, Nancy thought, was a real blessing. Certainly the rituals consumed time. Getting up, washing, dressing, making the bed, fixing coffee and toast, driving to work; all this kept the rats at bay and even the late afternoons weren't bad. Coming back to a clean, warm apartment was pleasant. Usually she turned on the five o'clock news while the tub was filling and even opening her mail and feeding the cat were things she enjoyed doing.

But sooner or later the darkness would fall. As the sounds of traffic diminished and faded away, and the people disappeared from the street, then, as though on cue, she would turn off the TV and sit in the old rocker by the radiator and stare back at all the dark rats as memories of the rapist returned.

Why does God permit filthy animals like this to walk the earth, Nancy would brood. Why do darling little innocent babies sicken and suffer, why do the just, the good, and the sinless die in car wrecks and cancer wards, in fires and floods and battlefields, while depraved creatures like Roosevelt Holmes were allowed to prowl the earth inflicting unspeakable pain upon other human beings.

When Holmes was in custody he had boasted openly of the thirty-four women and girls he had raped. One of them, a school girl of ten, was still in the intensive care unit at Methodist Hospital.

At six-feet-two and over two hundred pounds, he had savagely beaten a number of his victims and had bitten the nipples off at least six of them. On others he had broken ribs, smashed out teeth and at least once he gouged out the eyes of a nurse's aide who in her desperate struggle had ripped off his ski mask and gotten a glimpse of his face.

His first trial had resulted in a hung jury and when he was retried and sentenced to two years in prison, a flare-up of hostilities in the Middle East grabbed the headlines of the day and Roosevelt Holmes' sentence ended up a three-inch story on page twenty. Then, as the months drifted away, and then a year, the clamor and the talk diminished and the story was almost forgotten.

Almost.

Rather easily, merely by phoning the Department of Corrections, Nancy had learned the exact length of time a person had to serve on a two-year sentence less 'good-time.' A careful series of additional moves had enabled her to learn that Holmes had been a model prisoner, had indeed earned the maximum amount of time off for good behavior, and it was then relatively easy for her to pinpoint the precise date of his scheduled release.

If only Chris would get here. Chris had the strength, the guts, and the know-how to handle this thing right. Not getting a phone call didn't mean something bad had happened. Nancy knew that Chris was highly resourceful, that one move determined the next, and that no news no doubt really was good news.

But still, in only five days Roosevelt Holmes would be back in circulation. In only a hundred and twenty hours he would be back drinking in the bars, leering and scheming and prowling unchained once again in the midst of the weak, the innocent, and the unwary.

Pray God that Chris gets here in time. Nancy felt her heart squeeze as she rose from the old rocker, went to the closet, and from far back on the top shelf, pulled out a brown shoe box and carried it into the living room.

Opening it mechanically, she extracted the flimsey items within and stared at them almost sick with horror. Yes, there was the torn bra, just as she remembered it. And there were the ripped panties with the crusted brown stain which once had been warm red blood. And was it only her imagination or didn't the whole box reek of that evil odor she hated like nothing else on earth. That vile male smell that had come like the breath of Satan to poison the night and fill her heart with an all-consuming obsession to kill.

Chris had no idea that Nancy still had these grisly items in the apartment. Someday I'll burn them, Nancy thought, but not yet; not till it's all over with.

She replaced the shoe box on the shelf and going into the bedroom she threw herself down on Chris' bed and began to weep uncontrollably.

* * *

The Cheshire Cheese was bubbling and churning with activity when Savanna walked in a bit after seven o'clock. Working his way through the throng, he found a place at the bar and ordered a Bud.

"Quite a crowd you've got here," he said to the bartender; "is it always like this?"

"Happy hour," the bartender replied; "plus we have a couple conventions."

Savanna swiviled around and, sipping his beer, looked over the milling, somewhat noisy crowd. Over the sound of the organ coming from the next room they were laughing, calling out to others, talking loudly and obviously having a good time. Many of them wore identical white plastic hats and had a large VW badge on their lapel. Car dealers, Savanna thought. He wondered how they could find so much enjoyment in each others company.

The key to room 503 was in his pocket. As Martin Fox had said, a room had been reserved in his name. The clerk, after only one brief check, had handed him the key with no comment.

Savanna had not gone to the room. It still was not seven-thirty and he found himself wondering what George Gannon would be like and what he would have to say. He figured he had nothing to worry about. Certainly these people could never pose the threat that the prison authorities had. Out here there was no loss of good time, no forfeiture of privileges, and no solitary confinement. The worst they could do was perhaps mock him someway or another, or maybe abuse him verbally. Nothing worse. He wondered what they wanted from him and decided to hang back and say as little as possible until he found out.

Savanna turned back to the bar, ordered another beer and had just begun to pour it when he felt a hand on his shoulder. A voice spoke almost in his ear: "Hello, Vince, how are you!"

Somewhat startled, Savanna looked around quickly and saw an immaculately attired man of about thirty-five with wavy, wheat-colored hair and an enormous set of shoulders. "I'm Gannon," the man said. "Did you get your room?"

"Yes, sir, I've got the key right here."

"Good. Let's go up there and talk; it's a little noisy around here."

Savanna pushed his change onto the backbar and stood up. "OK by me," he said.

* * *

When they were alone in the elevator Gannon said: "What did you do all day?"

"Mostly I just screwed around," Savanna replied. "I poked around in some of the big stores—Dayton's and Donaldson's—and I went over to Power's and spent a lot of time in their book department. Then I walked down Hennepin Avenue and looked at some of the old familiar sights. Christ! that part of town is really going to the dogs. It's a regular skid row—in fact it's dirtier and crappier-looking than Washington Avenue used to be."

"The pimps and whores got to have some place to hang out," Gannon said.

"Yeah, I suppose. Say, Mr. Gannon, I understand you're my new parole officer."

Savanna was startled as the man burst out in genuine laughter. "No, no, no; not by a long shot. I've got nothing to do with those people. No more than Fox, the guy who drove you here to the cities."

"Well, who are you then?" They had

left the elevator now and Savanna was opening the door to room 503.

"I belong to the group that got you out of the joint. You're working for us now and I think you're going to enjoy your new job."

Savanna threw the key on the coffee table, lit a cigarette, and flopped down in a chair. "OK," he said, "let's have it."

George Gannon sat down carefully on the edge of the bed and seemed in no hurry to begin. When he finally spoke it was slowly; he seemed to be picking his words with considerable thought. "There are half a dozen of us in the group, Savanna. We're thinkers and doers. First we think and then we do."

"Do what?"

"Anything we feel like doing, especially if there's a lot of money to be made by doing it.

"Right now we're interested in making a movie about modern crime and criminals," Gannon went on. "We've got plenty of money but we really don't know much about the business—the business of crime— and we don't even have a story in mind at the moment. We don't have any interest in a re-hash of the same old tired crap—like bank robbers, love triangles, dope peddlers—none of that shit. What we're looking for is something really original and new. Something that'll grab the imagination of the American people and really give them a thrill. And something which'll make me and my friends a whole bunch of bucks at the same time."

"Where do I fit into all this," Savanna asked.

"You've got a devious brain, Savanna. We know that because we've got copies of your psychological profile, plus reams of studies and tests done on you over the years. On top of that you know a lot of criminals throughout the midwest and we want you to start sniffing around, full-time, and let us know what they're up to."

Savanna was alarmed. "Jesus, man, I'm no snitch; I could get myself killed real easy."

"No chance," said Gannon blandly. "You have to remember that we're not policemen. No matter what anybody's doing, we report nothing. For the simple reason that we honestly don't care. We're just looking for a twist, an angle, —something new. And when we find it we'll let you know and then you're off the hook."

"What hook? What can you do to me?"

"For one thing," Gannon answered levelly, "we did get you out of the joint. We can put you back just as easily. For another thing, we'll break every bone in your body if you try and give us any of your shit, and reason number three is that we plan to pay you damn good money for your cooperation."

Savanna was silent for a moment.

"How much?" he finally asked.

"How does two hundred bucks a week grab you!"

"Sounds pretty good. It's more than I'd take home working at some factory job. But what exactly am I supposed to do. Make a list of all the criminals I know and find out what they're doing?"

"Don't be making any lists. Just make the rounds—the bars and the hangouts—and keep your ears open and pick up as much as you can."

"How often will I see you," Savanna asked.

George Gannon had walked over to the window where he stood with his hands in his overcoat pockets gazing down at the traffic on Fourth Street. "You probably won't see me at all," he replied. "I've got some forms I'll leave with you. Fill one out every week and we'll mail you a postal money order as soon as we get it."

"A money order for two hundred bucks?"

"That's right. Every week."

Savanna was silent for some time. "How big an area do you want me to cover," he asked.

"Mostly the metropolitan area," Gannon said. "That's where most of the activity is. But don't hesitate to go out of town. Go north to about St. Cloud, east to about Hudson, south to the Iowa line, and as far west as you find anything interesting."

Savanna mulled it over. He knew this area well and in fact had been in—at least through—most of the towns. It beats hell out of making twine, he thought.

A new idea struck him. "Is it true I was picked by a computer," he asked.

Gannon laughed. "Oh, yes. You were picked by a computer, all right. But only because it had no choice. We fed it fifty-two of your personal characteristics and then just sat back and waited. It was inevitable that your card would be spit out. I mean, what the hell, man; we specified two teeth missing, shoe size, no scars or identifying marks, mild myopia, number of sibs, ethnic background, exact number of DWI arrests . . ."

Savanna was impressed. "You mean you asked for a guy who fit that bill exactly because it was me you wanted all the time?"

"Now you got it, kid. Shit! we even had your hat size. Seven and a half; right?"

"I guess so," Savanna said thoughtfully. "But I'm still not sure why it was me you wanted."

"Because you're a fucking jerk," Gannon said savagely. "You're a controllable high-grade moron who only looks out for his own ass and to hell with everybody else."

"That's bullshit and you know it."

"Is it? Why don't you go look in the

mirror sometime. And let me know what you see. I'll tell you what I see: I see a clown going on middle age who ain't got a pot to piss in. You've got no house, no car, no job, and no real skill of any kind. You've got no friends, no wife, no kids—neither chick nor child, as they say—and, for Christ's sake, you haven't even got brains enough to keep yourself out of the joint. Tell me, smart man, where were you and what were you doing just twelve hours ago!"

"I'll tell you one thing I've got, Gannon," Savanna said glumly, "I've got what it takes to tear your fucking face off any time I feel like it." He stood up.

Again Gannon laughed, a loud peal of genuine amusement. "No, Vincent, you can't even do that. But you're perfectly welcome to try. Come on! I'll move my hand six inches and turn your brains to mush."

"Your ass!"

"I said come on; I mean it!"

Savanna looked at him silently for a moment, then slowly sat down again. "All right," he said, "that part's not important. Not right now anyway. But I don't mind telling you that I don't believe a damn word you've just told me. I got no idea what your game is but I think this stuff about making a movie is a bunch of crap. Did you ever make a movie before?"

"No, we never did," Gannon replied.

"But we've done plenty of other things. Do you remember a couple of years ago when that guy got out of a Mexican prison on a helicopter that landed right in the prison yard?"

"I read something about it."

"That was us. We did it five times, all over the world. We called ourselves 'The Can-Openers' and we'll do it again, anytime, any-place—providing the price is right."

"You wouldn't shit me would you?"

"Sure I would if I felt like it, but I just happen to be telling you the truth when I say we know how to do things. There's a number of us in this club, if that's what you want to call it, and I state flat-out that, buddy, we are GOOD. We had a coke line out of Columbia that worked slicker than hot leopard shit till our plane hit the water but things were getting too hot anyway so we got out. Then we started bringing people out of Poland. Took 'em on foot across the Czech border and flew them from Vienna to Toronto and, boy, you'd shit little green apples if you knew how many we got over here. Today they're working in Chicago, New York, the west coast—all over the place."

Savanna was deeply impressed. He sat quietly now and said nothing.

"So you see, while you were busy making twine up there at the state prison, people out here were busy doing things. They were moving around, enjoying life, making money, and laughing out loud at suckers like you who think they're so goddamed smart. And on top of that they were fucking women day and night while you were beating your meat and only dreaming of pussy."

"And any time you want to question me or my friends, or doubt our veracity, or our ability to bell the cat, always remember one thing: we did get you out of prison—and that's something you couldn't do yourself. Right?"

"Yes, I have to admit that part is true," Savanna said. "I guess I owe you a thank you for that. And I'll go along with you as long as I don't have to do anything illegal. It's true I know a lot of sleezy cats. I dunno, maybe I can dig up some off-beat stuff. I'll see what I can do anyway. How long is this going to go on?"

"Five or six months at the most. If we don't find anything interesting by then we'll just move along to greener pastures."

"Then can you get me a discharge," Savanna asked; "there's nothing I'd like better than to be free of these corrections bastards once and for all—to be able to come and go and travel around as I please."

"Yes, we can get you a discharge," Gannon told him. "Better than that, if you come up with a real winner we'll get you a conditional pardon."

"Fine. That's great. Now how about let's adjourn this little meeting and go have a drink."

"There's just one more thing," Gannon told him, reaching in his inside jacket pocket, "take a couple of these forms we had made up and, as I told you, fill one out and mail it to us every Friday. Here's an envelope with our P.O. box number and correct zip code. We'll expect to receive it every Monday and we'll send you your two hundred bucks right away. That's not a whole lot of money, I know; you can't be running around playing big shot, but it'll keep you in eats and sleeps and you have to admit you've had worse jobs in your life."

Savanna chuckled. "No two ways about it. By the way, did you plan on giving me any money right now?"

Gannon reached in his overcoat pocket so quickly that Savanna knew the question had been expected.

"No, I didn't," Gannon said. "But here's a hundred bucks on general principles."

Savanna took the bill. "OK, then," he said. "I'll scout around and keep in touch with you and we'll see what happens. By the way, thanks for everything."

The two men left the room and walked down to the elevator without speaking. "No drink for me," Gannon said when they got to the lobby, "I'm a little short on time. Otra vez." The two shook hands. Savanna watched Gannon go through the revolving door to the street. Then turning, he walked back into the

Cheshire Cheese and sat down at the bar.

* * *

Dr. Avery Sachs crossed his legs and looked thoughtfully at the young woman seated across the desk from him. Until a moment ago it had been perfectly quiet here in his twenty-second floor office in the Crocker Bank Building on Sunset Boulevard. But now Nancy Rausch was sobbing. "I hate him so intensely, Doctor," she was saying in a strained, jerky voice. "I despise the bastard."

"Certainly you do, Nancy," Dr. Sachs said gently. "But please try to remember—and I've told you this before, dear—that this is a perfectly natural reaction. All of these feelings are authentic and normal and what you are going through has been experienced by many, many other women."

"I'd like to cut his fucking balls off!"

"I'm glad you said that—and again I do wish to remind you that I have told you more than once that this is a healthy and acceptable response. Fright, anger, anxiety, disbelief—all these emotions are to be expected. Have you contacted the people at the Rape Crisis Center yet?"

Nancy Rausch appeared not to have heard. "The worst part of all is that I'm so suspicious of everyone nowadays," she said. "For example, the fellows I work with—my

67

common sense tells me they're ninety-nine percent good, decent guys. They have wives and children and girlfriends and sisters and they work hard and wouldn't harm a flea. But I find I'm tense around all men now. All I can think about is that cruel animal thing they have between their legs and I hate them all for the pain they inflict with it."

"Nancy, I have really been hoping that you would enter the period of resolution. After all, it has been a while now. Let's see, it's been well over a year, a year and a half ago now."

Nancy's voice rose perceptively: "It seems like yesterday. It's all I ever think about day and night. Will it ever go away, Doctor? Do I have to live with this nightmare for the rest of my life?"

"Yes, you have to live with it, Nancy. I promise you that time will soften things but you have to do your part too. After all, other women have been through this and today they are living productive, reasonably happy lives and there's no reason at all why you can't adjust and carry on the same as they have done. We all have different capacities for absorbing pain, of course, but the human spirit is incredibly resilient and I can foresee the day when you laugh again and enjoy life as much as ever."

Dr. Sachs glanced at his watch and then said suddenly: "It's nearly lunchtime; are you hungry, Nancy?"

"Heavens, no; I couldn't eat a thing."
She dropped her balled-up tissue in the waste-basket.

"Did you have any breakfast?"

"No, I never eat breakfast; nobody
does."

"Sure they do. Come on now, let's pop
down to the cafeteria. There's nothing like a
little food now and then to pick up the spirit."

"Oh, all right, Doctor; I guess maybe I
am just a little bit hungry."

* * *

Later, over sandwiches and salad in
the bank cafeteria, Avery Sachs again tried to
suggest going to the Rape Crisis Center.

But Nancy would have none of it.
"There's nothing they can tell me that I don't
already know, Doctor, and besides, it's too
embarrassing."

"You're a very superior person, Nancy.
That's one of the reasons you find it hard to
respect anyone—even persons who, in some
areas at least, are truly deserving of your
respect."

"I respect you, Dr. Sachs; that's why I
come to you."

"But, Nancy, I'm referring to some of
these people at the center. Wouldn't you let
them try—just try—to make your burden a

little lighter?"

"No. I want the pain to go away but I want the hate to stay. I want it to stay forever and ever. In fact I want it to grow bigger and deeper and more fierce because, believe you me, someday, somewhere, somehow, I'm going to get even with that son-of-a-bitch Roosevelt Holmes if it's the last thing I do on this earth."

Dr. Sachs lit a Nat Sherman's cigarette and looked off to the distance reflectively. "How old do you think I am, Nancy."

Somewhat surprised, she looked at him a moment before replying. "I don't know, Doctor. Forty-six, forty-eight . . . not fifty, I know!"

Dr. Sachs smiled. "You're not even close; it's nearly twenty years since I was that young."

Nancy was incredulous. "They say it's not the years, it's the mileage," she said finally. "You must have had a real easy life."

"Not at all," the doctor replied easily. "You've heard of Auschwitz, haven't you."

"Yes."

"I was in the lower camp at Auschwitz for three years. Except for one sister, my entire family died there. My father, my mother, my older sister and my two little brothers. I survived, as did my one sister and believe it when I tell you it took a little doing. Not just staying alive during the war, but I'm speaking specifically of the years that followed; in some ways those times were the hardest of all."

Nancy said nothing. She had stopped eating and stared at Avery Sachs intently.

"I simply cannot tell you how I hated those people, Nancy. It was an all-consuming hatred much like that you feel toward Holmes. And it was also very self-destructive. When I grew to realize the extent that it was destroying me I resolved to overcome it. As a matter of fact, it was in an attempt to solve my own personal problems that my interest in psychiatry was kindled. I didn't initially have any intention of becoming a psychiatrist but as the years went by I became more and more interested in the field until, well, that's what I became."

Nancy couldn't resist asking. "And now you don't hate Germans any more?"

"They're not my favorite people but, no, I definitely don't hate them. My self-preservation depended upon reaching that stage of development and it was no Judeo-Christian principle that enabled me to reach it, but just a pure and simple, very selfish desire to survive."

"A little hate never hurt anyone, Doctor."

"Maybe that's true. But hate must either grow or die; it won't stay little. Do you think a three-inch weed in the corner of your garden can stay three inches tall? If you permit it to do so, hate will poison every cell of your body and soul. It will grow into the center focus of your very being and finally, absolutely, it will kill you."

"I believe you," Nancy told him, "but I don't care."

"I care," the doctor said; "I care very much. But all I can do is support you; I can't do it for you."

They had long since finished eating.

"Why is it you never send me a bill, Dr. Sachs?"

The doctor smiled at her. "For one thing, my dear, you can't afford me; is that reason enough?"

She held out her hand and new tears were glistening in her eyes. "I guess that's very true, Doctor. When I picked your name out of the yellow pages last year I had no idea what a psychiatrist cost. But I do thank you very much for the time and help you've given me."

"I'm not at all sure I have helped you, Nancy."

"Oh, but you have!" She stood up and took her purse.

"Call me anytime, Nancy; I'll always be here."

* * *

*(Not all of the cassette tapes re-
corded by Zeff and Eckman were lost with
the destruction of the Cohen farmhouse.
Those stored in a metal file box in the
kitchen were incinerated beyond salva-
bility. Some others however, along with
various small household items, were blown
out into the yard, perhaps in the first
explosions. And still more of them, some
very revealing, were recovered in a jacket
pocket and in a leather suitcase where
they had been buried undamaged when the
north wall collapsed.)*

* * *

Let the record show that this is March
first, in the year of Our Lord nineteen hundred
and seventy-nine. This is Charles Wayne Zeff
speaking and I'm going to chat for awhile with
Donald J. Eckman, a smart man but also the
most cynical person I have every known.

I'm not cynical, Zeff, I'm right. You
can't be both. If I tell you that three-fourths
of all cops have broken the law while on duty
you might be justified in calling me a cynic.
But if I lay documented evidence of this fact
right on the table then you're wrong in calling
me a cynic. Because I just happen to be
stating a true fact.

OK, then; you're not a cynic, Don;
you're a guy with a lot of very discouraging

facts. Tell us what you think of the United States of America, please.

I think it's the most fucked-up country in the history of the human race. I also think it's headed downhill every day—it's sinking lower and lower in the cesspool and it's absolutely, positively doomed. If I had any kids, I'd take them out and shoot them because they'd be far better off dead than to have to go through the horrible days that are coming.

Nothing in the Old Testament even comes close to the evilness that fills this country. You think Sodom and Gomorrah were bad? Shit, man, those towns were *nothing*—I mean nothing compared to what's going down today. At any hour of the day or night there're more cocks being sucked in San Francisco than there were on the whole earth in the olden days. Every hotel room in that town reeks of come and Vaseline. And I know what I'm talking about because I used to live there. Jesus! the place is crawling with fags; they're thicker than maggots on a dead cat.

And how about those animals in L.A. with their racks full of pornography, and their movies of dogs and donkeys fucking women, and their stores full of sex hardware, and the child porno bastards—to say nothing at all about the pills and all that shit that's floating around.

Yeah. This some country, all right. I don't have much use for communists, Zeff. I don't like the things they do. But their basic thinking isn't any more screwed up than ours. There's people in this country that have two hundred million dollars in the bank. As a matter of fact I remember when Mrs. McKnight died, the widow of the founder of 3M, and the paper said she left an estate of three hundred and twenty-eight million dollars. Now I'm telling you flat out that there's something radically, drastically wrong with a system that permits one human being to accumulate that kind of wealth. That's one of the things they never teach you in school—or at least they sure as hell never taught me—but you bet your ass there is plenty wrong with capitalism. Because the only way you can make money like this is to cheat other people--you can only make this much off other peoples' work and sweat and brains. So when you stop to think of it, you can't blame the Russians for hating us so much; for wanting to stomp us out. By God, we really *are* the bad guys!

Yes, the whole country is headed straight for hell. Even the stuff we manufacture is the cheapest, shoddiest crap on earth. When I was kid, Zeff, Japan was the junkyard of the world. I remember playing with toy cars and when you turned them upside down you could see they were made out of beer cans. If something said MADE IN U.S.A. You knew it was the best that money could buy. It was solid; it'd last forever.

Nowadays everything is just the reverse. The really good stuff all comes from Japan—cars, TVs, cameras—and America has become the junkyard. Everybody here cuts corners and tries to get as rich as they can as quickly as possible and with the least possible amount of effort. Doesn't make any difference if you order a new car or a candy bar or a meal in a restaurant, it's always the same old story; everybody tries to sell you the cheapest thing they can produce at the absolutely highest price they think you will pay.

Jesus H. Christ! such greed. It's every asshole for himself in America today, let me tell you, and without so much as a single thought, not even a pretense, of morality.

Like how about these Mormons out in Utah, for example. Did you ever listen to the Mormon Tabernacle Choir singing all their phony songs to God and Jesus? Christ in heaven, what a laugh! They preach all their lives about the evils of tobacco and alcohol and how using these drugs is an offense against the body, the temple of God, and yet these same fucking hypocrites peddle the shit in every drug store and supermarket they own. Shit! they feature the stuff right up front— they even have sales on it from time to time! So that ought to tell you everything you always wanted to know about Mormons but were afraid to ask. Their opinion of their fellow man is revealed every time they sell a bottle of booze or a pack of smokes. Here you are, filthy dog, gimme that money and here's your poison. Take it home and kill yourself. If you ain't a Mormon like us then you deserve to die; it says so on the tablets of gold. Fuck Mormons and every hairy pussy they slid out of. They make me puke. I wish the sea gulls would come back and peck their eyeballs out just as they were ringing up a sale on their fucking cash registers.

And these bar owners are another bunch of motherfuckers. For years I used to drink in bars and I was actually stupid enough to think that they sort of liked me. Hi, there, Donny, how's it goin' today. You're looking great, kid! What'll it be—the usual?

Yeah, Zeff, I actually thought that they liked me—that they considered me a friend. What a laugh! The only thing a bar owner wants from any customer is his money. All the smiles and jokes and bullshit is nothing but a part of the game he plays to get that money away from someone he personally considers a fool. That's right, a *fool*! Bar owners consider their customers to be utterly contemptible. They look down on people who drink and deep in their heart they mock and despise them.

You know what a bar owner really is? He's a legal dope peddler. The day that grass and shit and cocaine become legal you'll find them for sale right there on the shelf next to the Jack Daniels and the Black Velvet. That's the kind of hairpin a publican is—a guy that's just looking out for numero uno and fuck everybody else and his brother too.

* * *

It was a little after ten o'clock Wednesday morning when a guard in the farm machinery building at Minnesota State Prison walked up to Roosevelt Holmes and handed him a pass to the Training and Treatment office.

Holmes was neither puzzled nor alarmed. He was scheduled to be discharged the following Monday and he knew that it meant his caseworker wanted to give him a final interview. He had been expecting this pass for the last few days and had even spent some time anticipating the questions and phrasing some of his answers. There was a certain amount of danger associated with these discharge interviews. True, the board of corrections had already assigned him a discharge date, but this date could be changed right up to the last minute in the event of a serious breach of conduct. Holmes had never liked Robert Spacek, his caseworker, and he was instinctively aware of the fact that Spacek despised him. The man had a snide, sarcastic manner of talking that made Holmes tremble with rage. Thus far, on the half dozen or so occasions they had met, Holmes had been able to restrain himself by conscious effort but he felt that now, at their last meeting, Spacek might deliberately try to provoke him in order to be able to write a disciplinary report which would almost certainly cancel the Monday release date.

A short time later, having changed from his denim work clothes into a set of clean khakis, Holmes walked out of the factory and headed slowly down the long sidewalk toward the administration building. He put his hands in his pockets and shivered slightly in the chill March wind. Yes, he thought, this was definitely a time to play it real cool. Spacek can't do a goddam thing as long as I just sit there quietly and answer his questions politely. I'm a hundred and twenty hours from the streets—just a hundred and twenty hours. No sense blowing it baby; no sense to that at all.

He walked a little faster now. In half an hour this would be all over with; all I got to do is stay loose and be cool.

* * *

Robert Spacek, his feet on the desk, was leafing through a case file when Holmes entered his office.

"Sit down, Holmes," he said without looking up. After a few minutes he threw the manila envelope down and, leaning back, locked his fingers behind his head. "Well, Holmes, where do we go from here," he said.

"I hope to be discharged next Monday morning, sir," Holmes replied.

"And then what. Back on the old rape trail, eh!"

Holmes said nothing. This was going to be tougher than he had expected.

Spacek wanted an answer; his face became slightly flushed. "Is it back to your old tricks, Holmes? More sneaking around, stalking,—more of that white pussy in the park?"

"I'm all through with that pattern of behavior, sir. I don't have any intention of ever breaking the law again."

"Bullshit!" Spacek exploded. "A rapist who gets away with it will always do it again and again. He develops the habit."

"But don't forget, Mr. Spacek," Holmes said softly, "I got caught."

The caseworker was annoyed. "You got caught *once*, guy; the other times your got away with it—and we know for a fact that there were plenty of other times."

Holmes wanted it on the record clearly. "What's done is done," he said, "but I'm just telling you the truth when I say I've turned over a new leaf. After all, I haven't spent my whole life in the gutter. It was something I let myself fall into and now I've climbed out of it and I intend to stay out of it; that's all."

Spacek grinned. "You found Jesus, huh; is that it?"

The inmate relaxed a bit. "That's part of it. I've been attending church services for the past year and, sure, it makes me feel better—that's why I go. But I've done other things since I've been here to improve myself-other things besides going to church."

"Like lifting weights, maybe?"

"I like lifting weights, and it helped give me a better opinion of myself too. But I mean I joined the group therapy sessions voluntarily and I've also done a lot of reading. I've read every psychology book I could lay my hands on and it's done a lot to help me understand myself and other people too. Nobody forced me to do this. I did it on my own because I wanted to. And I joined A.A. on my own too. I've never done anything wrong in my life except when I was drinking and I wanted to put a stop to it."

Spacek seemed mildly interested. He put his feet on the floor. "How is all this new-found knowledge going to affect your behavior in the future, Holmes."

The inmate looked at the white man and wondered if he was sincere. He decided to answer carefully. "I'm not mad at the world any more, sir. I used to be. I was in a dead-end situation back when I was breaking the law. I was under a lot of sexual stress, I had a sick self-image, and I hated all women."

"And now you don't?"

"Not at all. In fact I've got a real good woman and she's stuck with me all through this and I appreciate her."

"That would be Denise Chappel."

"That's right," Holmes said, surprised that Spacek was so familiar with the name, "she writes to me every day."

"I'm aware of that," Spacek said, picking up the manila folder and leafing through it again. "There's nothing here in the record about any arrests for being a Peeping Tom or a flasher. Ever try any of that stuff, Holmes?"

"That's not my bag, Mr. Spacek. Guys like that are people who are timid and shy; they're scared of women. I'm not scared of women; I never was."

"All men are afraid of women," Spacek said flatly. "Women have the power to grant or deny men the greatest ecstasy on earth. This gives them a power men lack and so it's logical that men should fear them."

"If you say so," Holmes said quietly.

Spacek raised his voice. "What did you just say to me?"

"I said I guess so, sir," Holmes said quickly, "it does seem logical." He knew he had skated onto thin ice.

Spacek looked at him for several long moments as though trying to make up his mind about something. Finally he spoke. "Do you still have the ski mask you used to use, Holmes?"

Holmes felt his face get hot; he had not anticipated such a question. "No, sir, I threw it in the trash a long time ago." Seeing a chance to make a point, he went on: "Most people thought I wore that mask to keep from being identified. And that's partly true. But it's also true that I wore it because I was ashamed of myself. Does that make sense to you?"

"Everything about you makes sense to me, Holmes," Robert Spacek said. "I look at you and I read your record and I see a cold-blooded, psychopathic rapist who's caused more suffering in this world than any other ten inmates in the prison. I see a glib, shrewd, calculating, silver-tongued bullshit artist who beat the system time and time again and really doesn't have any reason to change anything. Not anywhere in your record have you ever indicated you felt even a speck of remorse. This is a trait that all psychopaths have. They're not capable of remorse."

"I am sorry, Mr. Spacek. God knows it even if you people don't."

"Are you! How about that nurse's aide whose eyes you gouged out. She was only seventeen. Are you sorry you sentenced her to a lifetime in the dark? Do you know she's been in a mental institution since you did that to her? Do you even remember her name?"

Holmes felt his palms getting wet. He clenched them and looked straight ahead.

Again Spacek shut the folder and threw it back on the desk. "I don't have anything else to say to you, Holmes," he said after a pause, "but please don't walk out of this prison thinking that you've conned the whole world because I promise you that you haven't. The next time you come back to this place we're going to keep you for life. And don't worry, there'll be a next time; I'll make book on that. There always is with people like you."

Holmes stood up. "Is there anything else, sir?"

Robert Spacek made no attempt to hide his irritation. "No, there's not; get your black ass out of here."

* * *

At four in the morning, hours before the weak February sun was due to rise, the pain in his right lung awakened Donald Eckman. For several minutes he lay very still and forced himself to breathe short, shallow breaths and bit by bit the pain subsided. It always did. But it came more often now-- sometimes three or four times a week—and Eckman knew the tumor was getting bigger, just as the doctor had said it would.

The old farmhouse creaked and complained in the gusts of sub-zero wind and Eckman wondered if it had started snowing again. Snow would make it tougher to get to town—and he knew he'd have to drive in today to get more fuel oil for the stove. The five-gallon can was nearly empty.

Lying warm and comfortable on a couch he had pushed into the kitchen, Eckman lit a cigarette and instantly felt the pain stab him again. Dammit! he ought to lay off these damn things. But what difference did it make; the damage was done now. His electric blanket was warm as toast and he had seven additional blankets on top of it. Ever since childhood Eckman had needed a thick pile of blankets over him in order to sleep. He liked the weight of them pressing down on him. It gave him comfort; almost like an embrace.

Again he tried to inhale but this time the pain returned with such intensity that he coughed and dropped the cigarette on the bed-clothes. This was bad business. Swinging his feet out onto the floor he snapped on the lamp, retrieved the cigarette from where it had rolled, and rubbed out the little glowing burn it had already made in the wool blanket.

No sense burning this place down, he thought. He threw the cigarette into the sink.

In the month he had stayed here at the farmhouse with Zeff, Eckman had already discarded whatever illusions he might have entertained about life in the country. He knew now that there was nothing romantic about it. Out here there was no casual dropping into a restaurant for a meal or a hamburger or even a cup of coffee. Here there was nothing except what you had provided for yourself. Every can of beans in the cupboard had to be put there, every drop of water had to be lugged in, and hot showers at any hour of the day or night were no longer to be had at the turn of a faucet.

But worst of all was this constant, endless problem of trying to keep from freezing to death. "My God, I don't see how those Indians used to do it," he'd once told Zeff. "When you think of how those poor bastards used to live in teepees in those howling winds all through the savage winter with nothing but little stick fires to keep them warm and not a bite to eat unless they went out and got it with a bow and arrow—it makes you have a lot of respect for them."

Zeff had left yesterday for his monthly three-day therapy session at the Veterans Hospital at Fort Snelling and wouldn't be back till the weekend. Zeff and his mental problems! he wasn't any different today than he had been twenty-eight years ago at Lackland AFB, where Eckman had first met him. He's the some old introvert, Eckman thought, still isolating himself from everybody, still working away at his far out, half-crazy novels, still the same skinny, humorous, likeable screwball he'd been in bootcamp when he was only eighteen.

How many thousands of hours had he slaved away at those ridiculous books? Jesus! he had twenty-six of them all typed up and stacked neatly in the old foot locker under his bed. Imagine! Eckman reflected, twenty-six books—and every one over a hundred thousand words long!

Well, at least the dumb bastard had managed to keep himself out of prison. Which is more than I can say, Eckman thought. The guy never had any real money in his life—and he probably never would have any—but, by God! he was halfway happy anyway so maybe he's better off than me.

And he didn't have cancer either, Eckman thought. The guy sucks away on the cigarettes twice as much as I do and yet the long finger of the Big C. had never reached out and touched him.

I wonder what he'd do if I set fire to his foot locker while he was at the V.A. and burnt those novels of his to a crisp. Wow! the little guy would flip out for sure! They'd have to toss him in a padded cell and keep him there forever if anything happened to his stories. Eckman chuckled out loud at the idea. He genuinely liked Charlie Zeff—and even the books he wrote weren't too bad—but in spite of that the thought of burning up the books was an amusing idea.

Eckman's feet were getting cold. He decided that since he wasn't going to sleep any more anyway that he would get dressed and light the small fishinghouse oil stove that Zeff had bought at the hardware store in town. The other stove, the one Zeff had moved down from upstairs, used a wick and gave off only a fraction of the heat the little tin one did.

Eckman had learned that the fastest way to get heat was to pour a cup of heating oil in the peep hole and light it with a twist of newspaper. This was somewhat dangerous for if one poured too much oil into the pan it would spill out all over the floor, burning furiously. Twice this had happened but both times he and Zeff had managed to beat out the flames.

Eckman, using a funnel, knelt down, carefully poured in the oil and lit it. Within two minutes the little stove was roaring loudly and, along with the first two feet of stovepipe, was cherry red. Now Eckman filled a tin cup with water from the two-gallon thermos jug, set it on the stove, and waited for it to boil. A cup of coffee would hit the spot.

Life in the country had its advantages, he thought. At least you didn't have to put up with the fucking winos and punks and all the screaming and fighting and the stink of all the cheap apartments he had rented in the big cities. All those places smelled the same:

mold, urine, and cabbage. Why do poor people always eat cabbage? Must have something to do with the old country.

But a guy could go goofy out here with no one to talk to. To say nothing of a life with no sex. No wonder those old mountain men used to fuck sheep. They say a sheep's gash is the closest thing to a woman's cunt you can find on earth. How was it that they say the old-timers used to do it? Oh, yeah, they used to put the sheep's hind legs in their overall pockets to keep them from kicking—or was it to keep them from getting away? What's the difference; I ain't about to fuck no goddam sheep anyway.

The water was already boiling. Eckman stirred in a scoop of instant coffee with a plastic spoon and continued to let his thoughts wander.

Maybe if I was twenty-one again I'd save up a couple thousand bucks and slap it down on a little place in the country. Use my G. I. Bill. Find me some half-ass decent farm gal and raise a couple crumb-snatchers and eat raspberry jam on my toast every morning and just kick back and enjoy myself instead of beating my head against the wall trying to chase the fast bucks in the big cities.

But what the fuck, who wants a life like that! Who wants to walk into a house and smell nothing but puke and baby shit for twenty years. And who in their right mind wants to fuck the same woman for longer than two or three months. Pussy wears out. Anyone who would jump in the rack with a forty-year-old woman has got to be some kind of a pervert. Christ, I'd sooner be dead!

Hell! why even think about it. It's too late anyway. For me the hayride is over. I've got cancer of the lungs. Just like my old man. The doctor said maybe a year at the most and, shit, that was before Halloween—nearly four months ago. Zeff didn't believe me when I first told him. He said: Don't believe everything those doctors tell you, buddy; half the time they don't know what they're talking about. Well, it was kind of hard to believe, but this time the doctors did know what they were talking about. They were right.

Eckman had been working in a pet store in Colorado Springs when the St. Patrick's Day card had come from Zeff. It said little except that he was living on a farm outside Minneapolis and working on a new book. Eckman thought it over for the next few days then quit his job, withdrew the $8800.00 he had in the Colorado First Bank, and caught a plane to Minneapolis. The next afternoon he got on highway 12 and hitch-hiked to the farm.

Nearly ten years had passed since the two men had wandered around Arizona and Nevada together but Zeff was delighted to see his old pal and had promptly invited him to stay as long as he wanted. That had been over a month ago, Eckman mused, and, dammit, I kind of like the place.

There was no shortage of things to talk about. Both men had been drifters and both had an endless supply of stories to tell. Zeff told about his job sweeping and baling scrap paper in a print shop, about his job at the meat packing plant, the furnace factory, the dog food plant, the amusement park, the bowling alley, the restaurants—a total of thirty-two jobs from Nashville to Seattle.

And Eckman, for his part, related his antics and adventures in the mining camps, the record business, the unemployment lines, and the bars and prisons and honky-tonks he had passed through on the long road here to Cecil Cohen's farm.

"What impresses me most about this place, Zeff, is that biffy out there in back; the outhouse. It's really something to see how fast the shit piles up in the hole. When you live in the city and get in the habit of flushing a toilet three or four times a day you never think twice about all the crap and piss that one human being produces. It's something you just never think about. But by God when you start shitting in an outhouse and that stuff keeps piling up, well, it's no wonder they were always digging new holes for the shitter every couple months down at my grandma's farm. There were eight or nine kids in that family and when you stop to figure it out, any ten people are turning out something like a ton of shit and piss every month.

"Holy Christ! think of what comes out of a city like Chicago every twenty-four hours. No, never mind Chicago, just think of what comes out of one skyscraper every eight hours when you've got a couple thousand people working there!"

When they got around to the subject of Eckman's diseased lung, Zeff learned the true reason that his old friend had come to Minnesota.

"No way in hell am I going to let them cut me up, Zeff; no way. And I don't want any of that chemotherapy, either. For the simple reason that it's nothing but bullshit; I know too many people that've had it and all it did was make them puke day and night while their teeth and hair fell out and in the end they died anyway. So all the drugs and radiation did nothing but run up the bills and delay the inevitable. Why drag things out when there's no hope. I say when your number's up face it like a man and cash out with dignity. Why beg and whine and plead and start grasping at straws when it's just a waste of everybody's time and money. Not me, man; not me. I'm going to show a little class."

"How about if the pain gets so bad toward the end that you can't stand it, Don," Zeff had asked softly.

"I'll never let things go that far,

Charlie. I've got a Bull Durham sack full of
cyanide pellets I took when I worked for The
Tombstone Silver Co. and I've got a glass
beaker of sulfuric acid in my suitcase and
when the time comes I'll drop the pellets in the
acid and when they start smoking good I'll put
my head in the fumes and take the deepest
breath I can and in two seconds it'll be all
over—just like in the green room at San
Quentin!"

"That's going to be kind of embarrassing for your family, isn't it?"

"What family; all I've got left is a
couple of brothers and sisters and they think
nothing of it if they don't hear from me for
three or four years at a time. They know I'm a
traveling man and sooner or later I'll turn up.
So as time goes by and I don't turn up any
more, well, so what! And I don't ever want 'em
to know that I'm long gone. That's where you
come in, Charlie. I want you to do something
for me. I want to be buried right here on this
farm and I want you to keep your mouth shut
about it and if you do that for me I'll give you
all the cash I've got left and not only that but
I'll even sign my G.I. insurance policy over to
you. That's at least a couple thousand in green
money, plus ten grand from the policy, so
there you are; you'll have enough loot to last
you a long, long time. You can write books till
the cows come home and never have to work in
a factory again!"

"But, shit, Don, I'll never be able to collect on the policy unless I send in a copy of your death certificate."

"I didn't think of that. Well, don't worry, I'll figure it out. Actually, all you have to do is call any doctor and tell them your friend died in your kitchen from over drinking."

"Are you crazy! They'll have an autopsy for sure and in two minutes flat they'll find out how you really died and then they'll charge me with murder. Bullshit on that noise!"

"All right then, just forget about the policy; I'm sorry I mentioned it. But I still have over eight grand on me and you can have it all-- all that's left of it, I mean--if you do things my way."

"What is it I have to do, Don?"

"OK, now listen carefully: as soon as old Cecil Cohen leaves for California I'm going to hire a big D-8 Caterpillar and I'm going to have this guy come in and dig me a trench about ten feet wide and twenty-five feet deep and maybe thirty feet long. I'll have some equipment company come out from Minneapolis so that none of these farmers around here will know what's going on. All people in small towns love to gossip and I don't want anybody to know what I've done, outside of you. We'll tell the cat driver that we bought a big fuel tank from a gas station they're tearing down and we're going to bury it and fill it with fuel oil before the price goes any higher."

"But what are you *really* going to do?"

"What I'm really going to do is buy a used travel trailer and winch it down into the hole and cover it with waterproof sheets of polyethelene and then fill in the hole and level it off and spread around the extra dirt and nobody except you and me will know it's there."

Charlie Zeff was silent for awhile. "So all right, you've got a trailer buried way out on a farm and nobody knows it; what's the idea? I mean, what's the point?"

"It's my *coffin*, man! Shit, I don't want to lie in a muddy hole with dirt heaped on my face and maggots crawling in my ears. I want to be sleeping on a nice couch with fur slippers on and a nice warm blanket or two over me. Something like the Pharaohs of ancient Egypt. They each had a nice, private tomb, and dammit, that's what I want!"

Again Zeff paused to think it over. "How are you going to fill in the hole, Don. It'll take you ten years to shovel that much dirt by hand."

"I'll rent a tractor in town, or from some farmer. One with a front end loader. I'll tell the guy I need it to put in a garden."

"How are you going to get into it if it's completely buried?"

"Don't worry; I'll build some stairs and a passageway and I'll have a trapdoor about eighteen inches square in order to get in and out of the place but I guarantee you that this trapdoor will be so carefully hidden that no-body, and I mean *nobody*, would ever stumble across it by accident. Even if the FBI was actually looking for it they'd have to tear up the whole farm before they found it. That's how carefully I intend to hide it."

Charlie Zeff's eyes narrowed and he looked at his friend for a long minute. "How did the FBI get into this thing, anyway? I've got a sneaking hunch there's something here you're not telling me. Am I right?"

Eckman laughed. "OK, there is. Better hang on to your hat, Charlie, because this might give you a little jolt. I mean I learned a long time ago that there's nothing I can do to change this fucked-up country we live in. But there's one little thing I *can* do: when the time comes for me to go and I climb down into that trailer for the last time, you can bet your sweet ass that I'm going to take a couple of rotten fuckers right along with me!"

* * *

Even as we were flying over Las Vegas I could see the yellow fringe of L.A. smog. It wasn't real bad, of course, but yet it was easily discernable, even at nearly three hundred miles. I wondered how soon the day would come when the filthy stuff reached all the way to Albu-querque, to Omaha, and finally to the Eastern Seaboard itself. I hope to God I'm dead and buried when that day comes, I thought.

My head was a little woozy from the five Scotch and milks I'd had. It always seemed that whenever I'd get on a plane I'd either drink nothing at all or else I'd get half bombed. It all depended on what kind of a mood I was in. If I was moody and scared and depressed I'd never drink a drop. But if things were going great and I was happy, excited, and hitting on all cylinders, then I'd scarf down the sauce one right after the other until my head talked by itself and my hands and feet acted like they belonged to someone else.

One thing was sure though: I certainly couldn't drink like I used to in Korea. Well, what the hell, I was young and tough back in those days and I suppose my liver didn't even know what kind of poison this was that I suddenly started making it filter by the quart. Actually, it was Southern Comfort. God, it was easy to drink; like warm molasses! If I started drinking today like I did back then I'd be dead in a week.

But a couple snorts on the plane was no big deal. Things were looking real prime and I felt a squeeze of excitement in my heart that I hadn't felt in a long time. It was good to be back in L.A. again. Back with the palm trees, the weirdos, the loose cats, and the people who *did* things. Screw the midwest and all the pitiful piss-ants that live there. Well, if someone was young and locked into a job and a mortgage then maybe you could halfway forgive them--or at least understand them. But anyone who has a choice of where to live and elects to spend their heartbeats in the cornbelt has got to have sawdust between the ears. Jesus! the winters alone would drive a saint to pot. Forty below zero, ten feet of snow, no sun,--only a masochist would choose to live in such a hellish place. Even the wild animals couldn't hack it. I read where eighty-five percent of all the fucking rabbits in the north never made it through their first winter. Say a prayer for Bugs Bunny.

But the most horrible part of the midwest wasn't the weather, it was the assholes who lived there. It would be bad enough if they were merely stupid; anyone can overlook a little stupidity now and then, but these creeps acted like they knew it all; like they had all the answers. Their way of life was the only way to fly, their church was the One True Faith, their children never touched dope, a penny saved is a penny earned, a stitch in time saves nine, the harder you work the more God loves you, and all the rest of that corn-fed bullshit that I had crammed down my gullet from Day One.

And the biggest dorks of all are these cunt-lickers who live in these ethnic towns. Sweet Baby Jesus! what a hilarious bunch of clowns. The men all think the same and talk the same and dress the same and they all have their pickup truck and their hundred and sixty acres and their fat wife with hairs growing out of her nose, and dammit, it's perfectly obvious to an outsider that they copy each other.

The women are the same, only worse. They meet in the grocery or in the parking lot after church or in the post office and they all go through their identical, proper, practiced, moth-eaten, tiresome routines. How are you. The husband. The kids. Prices. The weather. Then the smiles, the chuckles, the forced cheerfulness. It's all an act. Just a role in a very boring play. Usually the most interesting person in these hayseed towns is the town drunk or the town whore. At least they have guts enough to live like they don't give a healthy fuck--which is a lot more than you can say for the lemmings whose every act, word, or new pair of pants is carefully selected in view of what other people might think.

There were hundreds of these ethnic towns scattered around the midwest. New Ulm, New Prague, New Caledonia, Dublin, Warsaw, Moscow. Some of the Irish towns I sort of liked. At least in places like Vinegar Hill in Kilkenny the guys would buy you a beer now and then, even if they did start an argument and threaten to knock you on your ass five minutes later. But the German towns were another bowl of fish entirely. I simply cannot stand Germans. Christ knows I'm one-eighth German myself but that fucking air of superiority these people carry around is something that drives me up the wall. They actually and sincerely and truly believe that they're the red-hottest puppies God ever put on this earth and everybody else is just a dumb turd floating down the river.

Boy! didn't I used to have fun baiting those krauts! For a couple of years in the early 'Seventies I used to spend every weekend in St. Joe, a wiener-schnitzel town if there ever was one. Yes, sir, those were the days!

The first time I ever walked cold-turkey into their St. Joe stronghold was at the VFW bar on a Saturday afternoon. I ordered a beer and poured it and took a good look around. I know a German when I see one and now I decided to have a little fun.

"Hey," I said in a loud voice, "are there any krauts in this place?" There were about fifteen men drinking at the bar and, incredibly, every one of them raised his right hand over his head like he was a schoolboy answering a question from the teacher.

"Well, I just want you guys to know that I don't like krauts," I said. "And as a matter of fact I used to kill you guys for a living. Damn right! Uncle Sam used to pay me seventy-five bucks a months to blow the heads off people like you and you better believe me when I tell you that not only was I real good at my job but it happens to be only job I ever had that I really loved!"

You could have heard a pin drop in the place. They were genuinely dumbfounded.

Some of these guys, I was to learn later, had been drinking together on Saturday afternoons for fifty years and not once in all those years had a stranger come into their midst uttering such shocking pronouncements. Looking back at it, I think they admired my guts, my sheer, unmitigated gall. Because not one of them got mad. They sat there like bumps on a log, staring at me in awe--almost like they were half-hypnotized--and waited to hear what I would say next.

My beer was empty now and I casually ordered another, half expecting the bartender to give me a rap in the teeth and the old heave-ho. But, without a word, he served me and then stood there staring like the others.

I had no intention of disappointing such an attentive audience.

"What really wigs me out about krauts is their air of superiority," I said. "Now if Germans really were superior, well, then this is something I could live with. But the plain truth is that it just ain't so. There are lunatic asylems all over Germany and do you know what they've got packed in those places? German half-wits! Krauts who gibber like monkeys, krauts who think they're Napoleon, and krauts who wet their pants like a two-year-old. And there's tens of thousands of these creatures so don't be telling me about the mighty Germanic brain because I don't want to hear it.

"And how good is Germany at winning

wars? Twice in recent times Germany got up on its hind legs and tried to whip the world and both times you guys got the living shit kicked out of you."

Of course, I knew perfectly well that probably everybody in the bar was an honorably discharged American veteran, but sometimes I say things out loud just to hear how they sound and this was one of those times. I went on: "All I can say, men, is that I hope and pray you guys try it one more time. Please, just one more time. Because next time, I said, shaking my finger at an old farmer across the bar, "next time, mister, I WON'T MISS!"

The entire barroom exploded with laughter. "Hey, slow down, buddy," someone shouted, "That's the Post Commander you're trying to shoot!"

The place was full of catcalls, smart remarks, and genuine merriment. I joined in, glad to be off the hook.

Sometime later somebody called out, "For one thing, you never even *saw* a German soldier, much less shot one, or if you did you must have been two years old. How old do you want us to think you are anyway!"

"I guess you're right," I said, "but I was in Korea. What the hell, it's practically the same thing."

"You probably weren't in Korea either. It sounds like you've spent most of your life in a baloney factory."

Again guffaws and peals of laughter filled the bar. But this time, instead of joining in, I bristled slightly. "Oh, I was in Korea, all right; I guarantee you that much. Pusan, Wonju. Suwon, Seoul City, Yong Dong Po . . . I was all over the place."

"What branch," someone asked.

"Never mind what branch," I replied. "I was there and that's all that counts. I was help making the world safe for democracy. I was fighting my guts out day and night so you farmer-johns could sit and guzzle American beer on a Saturday afternoon like this."

Several of the men had bought beers for me by this time and I stared at the bottles and reflected on whether or not to toss in the one part of the story that was a hundred percent true.

I decided to risk it. In a softer voice than I had been speaking, and in an entirely different tone, I said: "And the most incredible part of the whole thing, gentlemen, is the fact that I didn't have to go to Korea. Not only was I underage, but I wasn't even a member of the armed forces. My brother John was. He joined the Air Force right after the war started and shipped out to Texas for bootcamp. His mother almost went frantic from fear and worry. I say 'his' mother because I was adopted. She raised me but she wasn't really my mother; she was my stepmother. Anyway, she never gave Johnny permission to sign up. But he didn't need

103

permission because he'd turned eighteen that summer and he was old enough to do whatever he wanted.

"Well, Dad had died about six years before this and Johnny was the apple of his mama's eye and when he came home on leave and announced that he'd been assigned to Korea, why, she wailed and cried and carried on like you wouldn't believe. She thought he'd get killed for sure over there and then, with Daddy gone, she wouldn't have anybody left to live for. There was me, of course, and my little sister, but like I say, we were adopted and that's not exactly the same as a blood relative. Besides, I was never really important to her; I was just someone who lived at the house.

"'Why don't you take his place, Chris,' she finally said to me. And right away, without giving it a second thought I said to her: "Sure ma, why not! I'm sick of hanging around here anyhow'."

I took a long swallow of beer and was vaguely conscious that the room had become very still. I also felt, sensed, that everybody somehow knew I was telling the truth.

"So ma sat down at her sewing machine and altered John's uniforms to fit me—a tuck here and a tuck there—and it wasn't that much of a chore because John and I were pretty close to the same size.

"So then, when Johnny's leave was up, I got an Air Force haircut, put on the uniform, put John's traveling orders in my pocket, and headed for Camp Stoneman, north of San Francisco. After I was there a couple weeks my number came up and I was put on a troopship bound for Korea and, hell, there was nothing to it.

"John had only been in bootcamp for less than two months and nobody knew anybody else once we got to Stoneman. It was mass confusion and, by golly, I fit in as naturally as a leaf in the woods.

"This wasn't the first time I'd done things like this for John. Once, when we were in gradeschool, John stole a toy dog from a big department store downtown and ma made me take it back and apologize to the manager for stealing it and raise my hand and promise never to steal anything again. The man said he'd call the police if I ever came in his store again and so for twenty years I never set foot in the place again.

"Another time, I built a lightning bolt generator for him--it used big leyden jars--and John won the second place ribbon for it at the state science fair. Plus he got his picture in the paper. Well, I could go on and on . . . like for example how it was me who had to deliver his paper route when it was pouring rain because ma didn't want him to get his feet wet.

"But this time--the time I went to Korea for him--this was one time I was doing something I really wanted to do. I'd never been away from home before and it struck me as a glorious adventure, something terribly exciting. I didn't have any experience with sex either, none at all, and I wanted to get out there where the action was. And I did too! You bet your life!"

A ripple of soft laughter swept the room but a few quiet conversations had started up now and I knew I had held their attention for about as long as I was going to. I polished off the last of my beer and stood up, "Give all these old boys a drink on me," I announced grandly, throwing a sawbuck on the bar.

"So long, you men," I called out a bit later, "I'm going to be heading down the road now but I'll see you all later. And thanks for your company."

There were numerous calls of 'take it easy' and 'thanks for the drink' as I left and I knew in my heart that for some reason or another these people actually liked me and I knew I'd be back.

But I never did tell them about what I had done out there in that mine field in Korea. I never told them that John's college education was paid for by the insurance money ma got after the government informed her he had been killed in action.

These people in St. Joe were pretty decent, and they were marvelous listeners when I'd start in on another one of my stories. But I never told them this part of it because it was just too damn risky.

Besides, it was none of their goddam business.

* * *

We were making our final approach into LAX now. The pilot switched on the No Smoking sign and I fastened my seat belt and looked out the window. I sort of wished it was night. God, L.A. viewed at night from five miles up absolutely has to be one of the most beautiful sights on earth. For as far as the eye can see the lights of a hundred cities wink and twinkle and gleam like a hundred million Christmas trees. I'd told people about it time and time again--how beautiful it is; how the whole New York area is nothing but a hobo's campfire by comparison--but I wonder how many believed me. It's something they'll just have to see for themselves.

But there were no lights now. It was about noon, sort of hazy but not real bad. Aha! there was the Pomona freeway--there was the San Berdoo-there was ol' 605--cripes almighty! the miles I'd driven on 605; I wish I had a nickel!

Half an hour later I was standing out on the sidewalk in front of the American terminal watching the hustle and bustle of all the cabs, buses, and people. I looked over at the Theme Building and calculated the odds of being refused admittance on account of the way I was dressed. Nuts to you people, I said to myself, your drinks are too expensive anyway. I decided to catch a bus to downtown L.A. Ten minutes later it came along.

How was I going to lay this thing on Nancy. She was going to flip her lid when I told her we had to go back to the midwest. She hated that place with a deep and purple passion. But it had to be done. I had my plan set up now, exactly as I'd wanted, and no way in hell was anything or anybody going to interfere with business.

Nancy was important to me. Not only was she the first person to ever go hog wild over the parts of my plan I dared tell her, but so intense was her enthusiasm, so instantaneous and passionate, that I knew at once there absolutely had to be many others like her. So it was Nancy, more than anyone, who was responsible for the once tiny seedling of my idea growing bigger and taller and stronger until now at last it was nearly ready to blossom.

And I needed Nancy to talk to, to interact with, to bounce ideas off, and even to argue with from time to time. The Bible is right when it says, "It is not good for man to live alone." I'd been alone too much and there's no doubt in my mind but that it's dangerous. When there's no one to talk to it seems like everything gets out of proportion. Little mickey-mouse annoyances, ideas, and fears grow to be giants. There had been times in my life when I'd been isolated for three or four months and I started getting goofy in the head. I'd break into sweats for no reason. A gust of wind would make my hands tremble. And the most insignificant inconvenience would drive me into a blind rage.

Yes, I wanted Nancy around when I started pulling the strings. And I wanted a lot of other people just like Nancy around too. I knew they were out there, thousands of them; all I had to do was find them. And I *would* find them. Mr. Savanna would, that is. He'd damn sure better find them! That's what I got the punk out of prison for.

* * *

I got off the bus at the Greyhound station and walked across Los Angeles St. to Cole's Restaurant. I liked Cole's. I liked their French-dipped sandwiches and I liked to watch Jimmy Barela, the bartender, throw ice-cubes up in the air behind his back and catch them in a glass. Jimmy had been on the same job for fifty years and was a good guy to kill time with for an hour or so. Then I'd call Nancy at work and have her pick me up. When we got to the apartment in Westminster I'd give it to her straight and with a little luck we might be all packed up and on the way to Minneapolis in a week, maybe even less.

I walked down the steps into Cole's and

there was Jimmy, same as always. "Hi there, old man," I said, "mix me up something with an ice-cube in it!"

* * *

When Charlie Zeff got back from the hospital Sunday afternoon he saw Cecil Cohen burning some trash in a barrel out by the trailer. Knowing that the old man was planning to leave for the coast in a day or so, he decided to walk down and chat with him. "Howdy, Ceece," he said, "still trying to set the world on fire, eh!"

The old man smiled. "Hello, Charlie; haven't seen you around for a couple days."

"Yeah. I was down at the V.A. Went down Thursday."

"Do those people do any good for you?" Zeff had told him about the group therapy sessions.

"Not really. But it's nice to take a hot shower and get cleaned up once in awhile. I know all the other people that go and I enjoy chewing the rag with them. We get our meals too, did I tell you that. Pretty good chow too."

The old man stared into the fire for awhile. "Charlie," he said slowly, "when you're down there with those people do you ever talk about the future? I mean, do you ever try to come up with some kind of a plan for yourself?"

"No, I guess not, Ceece. I think about it

once in awhile but nothing I ever planned ever worked out yet so I just quit making plans. I just live day to day and let the chips fall where they may."

"I don't mean to pry into your personal business, Charlie, that's not what I mean at all, but bless my soul! it seems a mighty risky way to live."

"It is. But it doesn't bother me because it's the way I've always lived. To me there's no such thing in this world as security. I found that out a long time ago. And so I quit looking for it. Right now things are sailing along pretty good for me. Did I tell you I had my brother ship me all my old book manuscripts? Yeah! I've got 'em all right up there in the kitchen. My idea is to go through all of them and pick out a couple of the most promising ones and polish them up and see if I can get something published. There's all kinds of small outfits that'll pay eight hundred bucks for an ordinary paperback. Who knows, I might get lucky. Anyway, that's my plan as far as it goes. I realize I can't stay here forever."

"That's right, you can't," Cecil Cohen said. "I haven't really made my mind up yet but I'm starting to think about letting the place go, Charlie. I'm not getting any younger and every time I visit my sister she's after me to sell out and move in with her. God knows she's got plenty of room. Herb died, I don't know, seven or eight years ago and both her kids are gone."

The fire had burned down now and Cecil poked it with a stick slowly and thoughtfully.

"It's OK if I stay here while you're gone, isn't it," Zeff asked, "me and Eckman?"

"Oh, sure, sure, that part's fine. In fact I'd much rather have someone here. So damn much vandalism nowadays. But it's just that I want you to realize that I might not be coming back. Not for long anyway. Like I say, I haven't actually made up my mind yet but it's a distinct possibility."

"You want to come up to the house and have a cup of coffee, Ceece?"

"Let's go in the trailer here and I'll fix us one. I'm out of coffee but I've got tea. You like tea?"

Later, in the trailer, Cecil said: "I wish I could be like you, Zeff. There's damn few people that are as carefree as you. In a way I could even say that I envy you."

Zeff drank some tea and didn't speak for some time. "I'm not carefree," he said finally, "but I trust myself to handle whatever is coming."

"Then why is it you have to go down to the head shrinker every once in awhile and I don't," Cecil asked kindly.

"I have a tendency toward severe depression, Ceece. It's no big deal. I'm in what they call the male menopause. Hell, I'm going on fifty years old. All men go through this thing. It's just that I'm at that point in life

112

where I realize that no matter how long I live I still have to face the fact that a big chunk of it is behind me. But it hasn't got anything to do with my basic thinking. My basic thinking is here to stay."

Cecil thought it over. "Didn't you ever think of saving a little out of all the money you've earned, Charlie? My Lord! with all the jobs you've had you must have earned all kinds of money."

"Sure I did," Zeff told him, "I've earned over a hundred and twenty-five thousand dollars the past twenty-years. All that just with my back and my hands in the factories. And I spent every red penny of it too. Let me tell you, Ceece, there have been kings and queens on this earth who never had the luxuries I've had. I've had thick, juicy steaks when the sensible people were eating macaroni casserole. I was buying a brand new winter coat when they were making the old one do. And I was lying on the beach at Waikiki when they were shoveling snow and salting the bucks away. So who cares if they're rich today and I've got nothing. I mean, dammit, give me a definition of *rich*. Does it mean green pieces of paper in some bank vault? Because if it does then I'm not rich. But think of the memories I've got, Ceece; think of the life I've led. I've *enjoyed* myself! The world is full of sick old people who have tons of money-- but what good is it. They'd trade it all for the life I've had. I've had all the good times and I've got the glorious memories and they can't take that away from me."

Cecil Cohen dug out his Prince Albert and started filling his pipe. "That's a great way to live, Charlie, but if everybody lived like that the world would come apart at the seams."

"It's coming apart at the seams anyway, and we both know it. Personally, I don't care if Russia drops an atom bomb on us tomorrow."

"If that happens, then those who planned for it will survive. You and me won't live through it but they will."

"Are you talking about those people out in Wyoming and Utah who have all that dehydrated food stored up? Listen: those people are the best friends I ever had. I figure they're just storing it up for me. If the hard times really come, like these people believe, I'll just march up to their storehouse and help myself. Food, water, medicine, anything I want; it's all there ready and waiting for me."

"Are you kidding! They'll blow you to Kingdom Come if you try to grab their stuff."

"Me? Sure, maybe. But how about the fifty million people in back of me. Just how many bullets do you think these stupid hoarders have! And remember, we've got a few bullets too. Not only that, but don't forget that the Army trained me as a master explosives technician. I went to school a long time studying this business and I've kept up with all the new developments too. I'll bet you there aren't a hundred people in the United States who can out-do me on fancy tricks when it comes to explosives. And I wouldn't hesitate a second, either; not if I got hungry enough.

"Figure it out for yourself, Ceece. A supply of emergency food is only valuable to the extent that other people don't know you have it. But, hell, everybody in the U.S.A. knows where the chow is stashed and if the time ever comes that they want it they'll simply take it. So there you are!"

Cecil Cohen laughed out loud. "I swear to God, Charlie, you do take the cake; you damn sure do!"

Zeff laughed too. As he stood up to leave he said, "When are you leaving, Ceece?"

"Tuesday afternoon. My neighbor Wirtz is driving me down to the Cities. I'm on the night flight. Got to economize, you know!" He chuckled and slapped Zeff in the shoulder.

"Drop me a card, eh!"

"Sure I will. Say! by the way, what's that Caterpillar sitting up in the yard for?"

"Oh, that. A contractor I know from the hospital asked to store it for a couple weeks. He's got a job for it somewhere around here but they can't start until they get the paperwork straightened out. He gave me a hundred dollars. You don't mind, do you?"

"No, no, no; hell no." He grinned at Zeff. "Not as long as I get my cut I don't!"

"Sure, Ceece, sure; that's fair enough."

"Go on with you, Charlie; I was just pulling your leg."

Walking back up the hill to the farmhouse, Zeff thought: that old man is just about as nice a human being as I ever met. I just hope he doesn't get in any trouble on account of that crazy damn Eckman.

* * *

The car that Nancy and I ended up getting from the drive-away people in Garden Grove was a big chocolate-colored Mercury Marquis. They had quite a few other cars to deliver in Minnesota but they were economy models and I damn sure wasn't going to bounce around in a Pinto for two thousand miles when I didn't have to. Spring was the ideal time of year to latch onto a car in the southwest that was headed north. All the rich cats, having sat out the winter, were flying home to up north now, their cars following them, driven by hired drivers like me.

I'd decided to take a drive-away, not to save money, but because there was no real rush to get to Minneapolis and I thought Nancy and I might make sort of a little holiday of it. I figured we'd take our time and if we came to an interesting place, some spot we wanted to poke around in for awhile, well, why not.

When I sketched out the route we planned to take, the man saw that we would be driving through New Mexico and he gave us fourteen dollars for the temporary license required to take a drive-away through this state. "Don't take a chance on not buying a permit," he told us, "because you're going to get a fifty-dollar fine if you get caught. Plus they'll make you buy a license anyway and you might even spend the night in jail."

"Oh, don't worry," I said, "I'd never do anything as foolish as that. Trouble with the law is one thing I've never had and I don't intend to start now."

So they fingerprinted me and had me sign half a dozen documents, which I didn't even bother to read, and late Friday afternoon we were batting along the San Berdoo, heading east. Just as we were passing the Ontario Speedway, I changed my mind about our planned route. "To hell with the southern route," I told Nancy, "let's take I-15 north to 70 and go through the Rockies. All the bad snow is gone now and it'll give us something to look at besides that horseshit Oklahoma and Kansas. Who needs those places!"

"Suits me," Nancy said. "Besides, that way we'll get to keep the fourteen bucks he gave us for New Mexico."

I was annoyed at this remark. "I would have kept it anyway. For God's sake, do you think I'd give those hair-brains fourteen bucks just to drive across their lousy state one time. Like *hell* I would!"

"How about the fifty-dollar fine?"

"I've got the fifty bucks, Nancy. But what's the difference. I wouldn't get caught anyway. I've driven across that state twenty times and no one ever stopped me yet so I'd have to be stupid to expect to get stopped this time. Never play the other man's game, Nancy; make him play yours. That's the only way you'll ever get ahead in this world."

Nancy laughed and snuggled up to me. "Yes, boss," she said.

So I took the I-15 turn-off and headed north to Vegas. Partly because I didn't want any hassle with the highway patrol and partly because it made driving so incredibly easy, I had locked the cruise control in at exactly 55 mph and now we were floating along soundlessly, Bach playing softly on the stereo.

It hadn't been easy getting Nancy to go along. But then again it had been very easy indeed. I was half smashed when she picked me up at Cole's but I had good sense enough to wait until the next day before letting her have it.

Her face had turned pale when she saw I was serious. "Chris, are you insane," she said, her voice trembling, "Do you actually think that I'd go back to that crappy place. I'd sooner cut my wrist."

"Don't get dramatic, Nancy. Summer is coming now and you know how you love to lay on the beach at Lake Calhoun and watch the sailboats."

Nancy started to cry. "But the memories, Chris; how about all the horrible memories. Isn't that why we moved out here. Didn't you tell me we were through with Minnesota forever!"

"We're *almost* through with it forever," I told her, "but not quite. The time has come to get revenge on those bastards. We're going to give them something to remember us by. Sure, we could go somewhere else and do the same thing but Minneapolis is the ideal place. I know my way around, we'll have all kinds of people to help us, and I know how things work up there. So that's where we're going whether you like it or not."

"Well, I don't like it and I'm not going," Nancy insisted.

But in the end she did. Willingly and gladly. Somehow or other the name of Roosevelt Holmes came up--it must have been Nancy who first mentioned him--and it wasn't long afterward that Nancy did a complete about-face.

At first I was irritated by the idea. "Dammit, Nancy, we haven't got time to screw around getting even with a two-bit shitbird like Holmes. I've got bigger fish to fry. I don't want to waste time and energy on the punk."

"But I *do*," Nancy said with great passion.

I was curious in spite of myself. What is it you want to do if I promise to get hold of

Holmes for you," I asked. I remember thinking that Savanna could probably find the guy without very much trouble if I specifically instructed him to.

"I haven't got it all planned out yet," Nancy replied, "but one thing I'm going to do for sure is make that animal scream the same way he did me and I'm going to give him something to scream about too." She had stopped crying now and her eyes were gleaming.

It was perfectly obvious to me that this was the key to Nancy's compliance so I didn't hesitate for an instant. "OK, love, we'll do it your way. You pack it in with that job of yours and stick with me till we see this thing through and I promise you I'll give you Mr. Roosevelt Holmes. I'll have him hog-tied and handed to you on a silver platter and you can do anything with him your little heart desires. Does that make you feel any better, baby?"

So here we were now, tooling north on Interstate 15, Nancy dozing, me quiet and pensive, and the miles drifting by. We stopped at Baker for gas and Nancy wanted to cut up to Death Valley and look around. "There's nothing to see," I told her; "it's just a waste of gas. Let's drive on to Jean and play a little blackjack at Pop's Oasis." I had $62,000 cash in the trunk of the Mercury and I figured we could afford to have a few games. There was a twenty-five dollar limit at Pop's so you couldn't lose--or win-- much but I liked the place and I figured it was a good spot to relax awhile before hitting Vegas for some real action.

We got to Pop's just after dark and stayed maybe two hours. Nancy got half a buzz on drinking pina coladas and dropped eighty bucks in the slots. I was ahead about two bills at the table at one time but then I started playing three hands and a run of bad cards ate it all up along with about sixty bucks more. It didn't make any difference. Las Vegas was only thirty miles away and as soon as we got a room I planned on taking three or four grand to the tables at the Four Queens and see what I could do.

As fate would have it, we stayed in Vegas longer than I had intended. It was Sunday morning before we found ourselves out on the road again, Nancy with a splitting headache and me with $3900.00 of Nevada's money in an envelope in the glove compartment. Right from the start Lady Luck had smiled on me. I quit the Four Queens when I was $2400.00 ahead, walked across the street and picked up another $800.00 at the Golden Nugget, and then took a cab out to the strip where at one time I was $17,000.00 ahead shooting craps at the Sahara before I started cooling off. So I called it a day. The car was due in Excelsior, Minnesota at five o'clock Wednesday and I didn't want to get it there late. No sense attracting any unnecessary heat, I thought.

At Beaver, Utah, Nancy woke up and lit a smoke and said to me: "What is is that we're going to do in Minneapolis, Chris?"

"I don't want to go into it right now," I told her, "There's time enough for that later."

"But I *do* want to go into it right now," she came back. "After all, if I'm a part of it it seems to me I have a right to know what's going on."

She was right. "All right, I'm going to bring them to their knees. I'm going to knock out their electrical power and I'm going to poison their water supply."

Nancy's eyes got very round. "Why, Chris?" she asked simply.

"Because they're evil people," I said. "They're pawns of Satan. They never did anything to me but shut me out and mock me and I'm not leaving this planet earth until we balance the books. You've got to realize, Nancy, that I'm forty-five years old. I'm way too old to ever get anywhere in this world now but I still have all my wits and I still have my strength and I'm going to use what I've got left to mow down some of these fat cats before I cash out." Suddenly my rage was gone and when I spoke again it was almost reverently: "And after this I saw another angel coming down from heaven having great authority, and the earth was lighted up by his glory. And he cried out with a mighty voice, saying, 'She has fallen, she has fallen, Babylon the great; and has become a habitation of demons, a stronghold of every unclean spirit, a stronghold of every unclean and hateful bird, because all the nations have drunk of the wrath of her immorality, and the kings of the earth have committed fornication with her, and by the power of her wantonness the merchants of the earth have grown rich.

"And the kings of the earth who with her committed fornication and lived wantonly will weep and mourn over her when they see the smoke of her burning, standing afar off for fear of her torments, saying, 'Woe, woe, the great city, Babylon, the strong city, for in one hour has thy judgment come'."

From then on we drove in almost total silence for nearly four hundred miles. For there was little to say, but a great deal to think about. Tomorrow would soon be here. The day of reckoning was fast approaching and this thing had to be done right the first time because I knew we'd never get a second chance.

* * *

Vincent Savanna rented a sleeping room in the Kenwood area, bought himself some flannel shirts and corduroy pants at Kaplan Bros., on Franklin Ave., and started prowling the city. Almost immediately, in a Third Avenue bar, he ran into Augie Tangelo, a New Jersey crib man he hadn't seen in three or four years. "Augie! What the hell are you doing back here; things too hot for you back east!"

"Hi, there, Vince," Augie grinned, shaking hands, "Naw, I'm just kind of looking around. I like it here, no kidding, I really do."

"Bullshit! that ain't the way you talked when you were making twine. The way I remember it you said you'd burn in hell before you ever set foot in Minnesota again."

"Did I say that? Well, well, well; imagine!" Both men laughed.

Savanna remembered Tangelo as a super sophisticated safe-cracker with authentic mobster connections in the Jersey area. The gang he was with opened safes from Maine to Florida and there was nothing they couldn't open until IBM came out with their round-door floor job. Try as they would, Tangelo and his boys couldn't take this baby. They couldn't peel it, crush it, burn it, drill it, or blow it. They tried everything and it thwarted their every effort. Finally, in desperation, they sent out the word coast to coast that they'd pay five grand cash for an intact IBM round-door in-the-floor and in time the right connection was made. A new supermarket in St. Paul was scheduled to install one on a Sunday morning and Augie Tangelo, along with another man, drove non-stop from Atlantic City in a new, white T-Bird.

Sure enough! The safe was installed on schedule and several yards of fresh cement poured around it while Augie and his pal kept track of progress from a distance. That night, shortly after dark, they made their move. They backed a stolen tow-truck right through the big, plate glass window of the super-market, threw a chain on the IBM, yanked it easily out of the still-wet cement, and were long gone before the first sirens sounded. Half an hour later they had the safe in the trunk of their T-Bird and were on their way home to Jersey, where they intended to dismantle it at their leisure and learn how it was constructed.

But fate had other plans. After five hours on the road, the two stopped for coffee in a one-horse town just north of Milwaukee. Someone, seeing this flashy, out of town car with its tail dragging—in this unlikely place at such an odd hour—was suspicious enough to jot down the license number and, although it took time, Augie eventually ended up at Stillwater Prison in the same shop as Savanna.

"So what's happening, Vince," he asked now. "Got anything going?"

"I've got something going," Savanna replied, "but I'm not sure what it is." He brought Tangelo up to date on the events he'd been part of recently and Augie seemed very interested. "This thing sounds well organized," he said thoughtfully. "Keep in touch with me on it; I'm a great believer in what can be done when people are organized."

Savanna believed him. Tangelo finished his drink and hurried off a short time later, saying he had an important appointment, but not before telling Savanna he was staying at the downtown Holiday Inn. "Phone me or come over anytime," he said, "I'm here alone and I'll be around for two or three weeks."

Savanna made a note in a small tablet he carried and continued roaming about the city. He picked up at least half a dozen names and bits of information every day and by the end of the week he had enough to half-fill his little book. He copied everything down for George Gannon, mailed it, and wondered if his check would come on time.

There was no check. Just a white envelope with two one hundred dollar bills folded inside a plain piece of paper. Savanna pocketed the money and went back out on the streets.

* * *

It was a chilly afternoon and not many children were in the park but Holmes decided to wait around and see what turned up. He was sitting in a nondescript Dodge sedan he had purchased three days earlier and now he was parked on Willow Street, watching the activity in Loring Park. Years back this had been his favorite hunting rounds but times had changed and now it was almost the exclusive domain of gays. What few children he saw were not alone, they were watched over by adults hovering nearby or else they were accompanied by other children, ten and twelve years old, who were far too smart to be fooled by the sack of candy he had open on the seat beside him.

A young woman strolled by holding a delicious looking child of about five tightly by the hand. Paranoid bitch, Holmes thought angrily. He gazed after the child hungrily. From time to time he put his hands on his crotch and fondled his testicles. Come on, come on, he whispered hoarsely; come on over here you little mutherfuckers, I got to have me some ass.

Suddenly a light-skinned Negro girl of about eight came running toward Holmes' car pursued by a younger boy. Both were running at full speed and both were laughing merrily at the fun of their game. "Hey, there, little sweetie-pie," Holmes said, opening the car door and making himself laugh along with her, "You must be the fastest runner girl in the whole world."

The girl stopped and grinned at Holmes shyly. She was about ten feet away from him. "That's my brother, Adrian," she said, "but he can't catch me because I'm seven and a half and he's only six."

"I never, never, never saw a pretty little girl run as fast as you. I think you deserve a prize." He looked around quickly, not missing a thing. Two gays were kissing on a bench not far off but it was a good bet they hadn't noticed him. A middle-aged woman that Holmes thought had glanced at him earlier was still too near for comfort but she was bending over a toddler now, shaking her finger and apparently giving a scolding.

"Here's a nice piece of candy for my pretty little friend who can run so fast," Holmes said, holding out a large pink gumball. His groin ached now and he could feel seminal fluid oozing from the end of his throbbing penis. The girl smiled with pleasure and came toward him at once, her hand extended.

Suddenly her younger brother came screaming up from where he had been standing off to the side and slapped the girl's outstretched hand. "Mama say don't never, *never* talk to no stranger," he shrieked; "Mama say big men with candy is devils and we 'posed to run call the police. Help, help, HELP," he howled, "Bad devil man got candy, we wants the police, police. Help, help, po-leece!"

The two children scampered off at top speed, the boy still screeching. Holmes cursed out loud. "Goddam crazy little fucker." From the corner of his eye he saw the older woman who had been scolding the child turn and begin walking quickly toward his car. His hand was sweaty as he twisted the key and heard the motor roar to life. Both rear tires squealing, he tromped down on the gas and fled.

* * *

Holmes drove to a black bar near the courthouse, drank three vodka martinis in rapid succession, and sat listening to James Brown on the juke. He had calmed down now. That was some bad shit back there, he admitted to himself; I got to be more cool. He ordered another drink and sat thinking. The seed of a new plan had sprung up in his mind and he sat very still now, turning his glass slowly while the plan took on shape and dimension and the tingle in his testicles flooded his groin with warmth. He made a sudden decision, gulped the remainder of his drink, then left and hurried to his car.

Carefully, obeying all the rules of the road, he drove to the giant Hi-Lake shopping center on twenty-seventh and Lake. He parked in a corner of the huge lot, slid over to the passenger side, as though he were waiting for the driver to come out, and sat watching. Holmes knew that people with new cars often parked on the outskirts of lots in order to minimize the chances of their getting dented and for some reason or other he knew that the woman he wanted would be driving a new car.

He was right. In less than ten minutes a bright new yellow Sunbird pulled up not far from him and a willowy young woman got out, her wavy blond hair tumbling to her shoulders. She looked about twenty-three and wore a light blue jacket with white slacks. Instantly, Holmes moved over behind the wheel, started his car, and drove up beside her. He wanted to get her while she was between the two cars rather than out in the open parking lot. He saw he had plenty of time. The woman, with her door wide open, bent back into her car and Holmes, coming around his car from the front, saw that she was reaching for an infant, wrapped in blankets, lying on the front seat. In his left hand Holmes carried a silver lunch pail in which he had packed two bricks and then wired tightly shut. "Nice day, isn't it," he said.

The young woman turned toward him and gave him a smile showing perfect teeth. "It's a lovely day. I'm just so happy that . . ."

Holmes swung the lunch pail then and three of the girl's teeth flew out as it caught her on the right side of her face and shattered her jaw. She collapsed in a heap but still she remained conscious. "My baby," she moaned, her fingers opening and shutting convulsively, "my baby."

Holmes looked around swiftly and, seeing no indication that anyone had observed them, lifted the young woman and pushed her on her back across the front seat. With a slap of his hand he knocked the baby onto the floor, where it began to fret and wail.

"Fucking bitch, get that pussy out here where I can have it." He thrust his right hand under the waist of her slacks and ripped downward savagely, tearing off both her slacks and her panty-hose at the same time. Now he threw himself on top of her, fumbled in his pants briefly, and then rammed his engorged penis deep into her with a furious hatred again and again while the blood from her face smeared over him and her fingers clenched the air feebly until, with a final savage thrust, he froze in orgasm . .. and then he was done.

The baby was crying loudly now. Holmes slid off the woman, zipped up his fly, and then opened the woman's purse and took out a small package of tissues. Taking a number of them, he wiped off some of the blood from his face and then rolled them in a ball and stuffed them in the baby's mouth. "Chew on that, asshole," he said.

Holmes was nearly ready to leave. "What's your name, whore," he asked.

"Marlene," she whispered weakly. "Why did you . . ."

In that instant Holmes made the decision. Reaching in his pocket he pulled out a knife and snapped open the longer of its two blades. "Hate to do this, mama, but fucked if I'm gonna take any chances with you."

"Oh, no, please, God," the girl cried, "On such a lovely day . . . ohhh, my baby . . ."

Holmes raised the knife over his head and with a single powerful stroke stabbed her once in her heart. She died instantly, her eyes still open.

Moments later he was in his car and driving out of the lot onto Lake Street. When he was six blocks away he began to grin and the tight, hard words came out: "Fuck you, Robert Spacek," he said.

* * *

It was Nancy, not I, who first spotted Roosevelt Holmes at one of our early C.O.B.R.A. meetings. Although I had spoken for at least twenty minutes that night, and in spite of the fact that there were hardly more than twenty-five people in the audience, I never noticed him sitting there listening in the back of the rented hall in northeast Minneapolis.

But Nancy recognized him as soon as he walked in. When I finished speaking and walked off the stage she grabbed me by my arms and her face was ashen. "Holmes is here," she said fiercely; "In the back row, on the left." I put on my glasses and looked out around the curtain to the back of the rather dimly-lit, smoke-filled room.

"You're right," I said, "it's him for

sure. But let's just cool it for now. Let things ride. I don't want to create any kind of a scene with all these people around."

"Are you crazy, Chris; let's get him right now while we have a chance."

"I said *no*," I replied sharply. "This is neither the time nor the place. If he came once he'll come again. Savanna must know where he lives. He must have run into him and invited him here. Trust me, Nance, honey," I said, putting my arm around her; "all things come to those who wait."

* * *

Roosevelt Holmes committed his last crime in, of all places, St. Cloud, Minnesota, a heavily Catholic town about sixty-five miles northwest of Minneapolis. Parts of the story we got by going back through the newspapers of the week it happened, other parts we got from Amy Upton, who eavesdropped on a number of long-distance calls while she was working at the telephone company there at the time, but all the fine details we got from Holmes himself after we caught him. Under the circumstances of our quiz session concerning the matter, Holmes spoke very openly of the crime.

Apparently, this is what happened:

Four days after murdering Marlene Joice, Holmes drove to St. Cloud in anticipation of finding a college girl to rape. He knew there were thousands of them there, students at St. Cloud State. He began drinking in the early afternoon, moving around from bar to bar, waiting for the kids to start circulating after the last classes finished.

But by late afternoon the cold drizzle that had been falling all day turned to snow and in less than an hour nearly two inches had fallen, making the streets slippery and dangerous. By six-thirty the bars and pizza joints were nearly deserted and Holmes realized that the nasty weather would keep everyone home for the night.

Furious at this turn of events and seething with sexual energy, Holmes was driving along Second St., about to start back to the Cities, when he saw something. Stopped for a traffic light, he saw a blue station wagon pull into an Exxon station across the street from him and a man and young boy get out. The two entered the station and the man got a key from the attendant and handed it to the boy, who then came out and went around the side of the building while the man remained inside.

Instantly, Holmes acted. Making a sharp right turn he drove half a block and parked in the deep shadows of the side street. He shut off his engine but left the key in the ignition and his door unlocked. Then walking as fast as he dared, nearly running, he went

minutes passed before he was rational enough to realize the child's genitalia were still in his mouth. Rolling down his window, he spat the living tissue out onto the snowy road and then rinsed out his mouth with a pint of Vodka he had under the front seat.

An hour later he reached Robbinsdale, just outside Minneapolis. He was relaxed now and again he messaged his testicles as he drove. "Ahhh," he moaned blissfully, "Ahhh-h-h."

* * *

Of course, Nancy and I weren't even in Minnesota when this happened. We were probably somewhere out in Colorado, still coming this way in the Mercury. The crime created quite an uproar, especially in the St. Cloud area, but we probably never would have heard about it, and it never would have affected us personally, if Amy Upton hadn't brought it up shortly after she joined C.O.B.R.A.

I remember Nancy listening with fascination as Amy told us what she knew and it wasn't much later that Nancy told me what she had in mind for when we eventually got our hands on Roosevelt Holmes.

"You mean it, don't you," I said, impressed by her grim determination.

"I mean every word of it, Chris."

136

Even then I believed her. There was no need to say more but I knew for a certainty now that of all the crimes Holmes ever committed, his crime against little Hans Butterfield was the one he was going to regret most.

* * *

The first thing I did when we got back to Minneapolis was stop down at E. F. Hutton Co. to find out what was getting hot in the commodities game. It turned out that silver was easily the most glamourous thing moving so I bought ten lots for December and put up the required eight percent out of the cash I'd brought with me. December silver was eight dollars and some cents that day, nearly nine, so the $45,000 I had to post left me with only a bit over twenty grand, but I figured that would do me for the time being.

I'd been buying and selling commodities ever since I returned from the Far East back in the early 'Fifties. I bought and sold cocoa, tin, pork bellies, eggs, quicksilver, you name it; at one time or another I'd owned a little of everything. I guess if I'd ever known what I was doing I would never have gotten into the the racket in the first place because commodities is definitely a very risky business. But I never knew beans about any of it; I was strictly a hunch player and over the years I was amazingly lucky. A number of people who knew what I was doing said I was the nerviest bastard they'd ever known, that I was cold as ice. And it's true enough that I made some cool moves. In a rising market I'd sell everything, often at an enormous profit, and immediately throw everything back into buying three and four times as many lots of the same thing I'd just sold, gambling that the item hadn't peaked. In a bear market, where I'd sold short, I never waited for the cycle to bottom out. I'd buy fairly early, hang on to my winnings, and then try to catch it again on the upswing. Sometimes I guessed wrong, but not often.

It was an easy way to make money, no two ways about it. It beat the hell out of working for a living, anyway, and it made the gamblers of Las Vegas, by comparison, seem like silly little children playing tiddly-winks.

* * *

C.O.B.R.A., "Cabal of the Book of Revelation Angels", that's what we called ourselves. Even in my wildest imagination I never dreamed that we'd go as far as we did and who could have predicted, or anticipated, the turns that events would take. Only a madman would believe he could manipulate other people to obtain exactly what he wanted and whatever else I was I certainly was not insane. Angry, yes; disillusioned, yes; determined, yes; but not crazy. No, I had my general plan but I never attempted to spell out every detail, choosing instead to rely on my resourcefulness to solve problems one at a time as they arose.

I have always felt that failure to develop a child's ingenuity was one of the meanest things a parent or teacher could do to a kid. How marvelous, I thought, if someone would devise a number of games in which a child sought to achieve a simple goal and then, by loving design, was deliberately frustrated in his attempts to succeed. The child would be encouraged to seek new means to his end and would be graded and rewarded in relation to the extent that he used his imagination. I've seen cats try ten ways to get out of a house when they were in heat, I've seen a dog attack from a dozen different angles, and I've seen a grown man beating his head against a stone wall for twenty years, never thinking to try getting what he wanted by using a different approach.

Life is not fair, nor was it meant to be. Certainly life conspires to give some children more advantages than others. And it seems the greatest advantage a child can have is, ironically, not a childhood of soft beds and hot meals, but a life of hardship, deprivation, hunger, pain, and tears. If it kills him, well, so much the better for the species. But if he survives, as I survived, then the plump, soft marshmallows have no chance against him, no chance at all, for he has learned all the tricks. He knows how to adapt, how to slip and slide, how to suffer, to wait, and to calmly endure.

And best of all he develops an enormous confidence in himself. He is unafraid of strange people, unfamiliar places, or new experiences. He knows there is no such thing as security and so he does not seek it, preferring instead to rely on his own ability to be any kind of man he has to be in surmounting any crisis. Success feeds upon success and nearly a quarter century of not worrying about anything had served me well, or at least I felt it had, and starting C.O.B.R.A. never involved any trepidation on my part. Certainly it had a grander scope than any other scheme I'd designed, but I was ready for it now and everything I'd done before only seemed like part of my training.

I never had Savanna round up all the ex-cons and the street people because I wanted to merely use them. I did it because they would be eager listeners to what I had to say, because they already believed in their hearts what I was merely articulating, and because I wanted to see what effect it would have on me when larger and larger groups of people began applauding me. Was I perhaps secretly doubtful of some of the beliefs I was so forcefully expounding? Yes, maybe I was. It's possible.

But it's far more likely that I was simply too lazy to sharpen my skills in what you might call 'the market place'. Rather than start at point zero with intelligent, open-minded people, I chose to start with those I knew would agree with me because I wanted this advantage in attempting to get as powerful as I could as quickly as possible.

I told Savanna to spread the word that we'd have beer and ribs, and we did, but it wasn't until after we started making small loans, usually about twenty dollars each, that we developed a substantial turn-out at our meetings. A surprising number of people paid us back and this part of the program proved to be far less expensive than we had expected.

Naturally, the police knew all about us. Maybe at first they didn't, but it didn't take them long to start keeping track of us, although I will say they never actually gave us any trouble--at the beginning, that is.

My early speeches were off-the-cuff and quite short, rarely more than twenty minutes. Later, when I'd learned to dominate a crowd, to play with them, to tease and lead them, then I would sometimes go on for well over an hour. But in the early days I simply tossed them my street-wise philosophy as I had learned it over the years.

* * *

*Goodbye, America! Farewell to your sunny days, your laughing children, and all your might-have-beens. You gambled with the devil and the devil won. And now it is time to pay. I'm not going to get maudlin and go into a long, tear-soaked rendition of the beauty that once was because we all know how it used to be and how it was meant to be. There was a time when this country was the greatest country on earth. Sure, there has always been sickness, poverty, and hunger here but I'm speaking of the days—and they weren't all that long ago—when this country was populated by what were essentially decent, God-fearing, hard-working people. They plowed and planted the land, they built schools for their children, they attended church together on Sunday, they set something aside for a rainy day, they stuck together in times of peril, and it *worked*! You bet it worked! In only seven generations we rose from absolutely nothing to become the richest and most powerful nation in the history of the human race.

And then something went wrong. The big, wonderful machine called America started breaking down. Rivets popped, pistons broke, gaskets blew, and a horrible howling was heard as the stink of her dying filled the land.

Everywhere I look I see greed and filth. I see Satan victorious as IUD devices break sales records, as forests are destroyed to print tens of thousands of tons of pornography, as alligators gorge themselves on dead fetuses in the slimy sewers of New York City. I see God forgotten, hope abandoned, and I see Four Horsemen riding down upon us.

Make no mistake about it, these are the end times. The Apocalypse is real; it is upon us. Now!

Is there a politician who can save us? No, the body is too sick, too far gone to be healed. The warring factions can never be brought together in the time remaining. So ignore the strident screeching of the clowns on the band stand; they can't even save their own ass let alone anybody else's. Their promises are nothing but self-serving lies. What would you think of a doctor who told a terminally ill patient that there was nothing to worry about; that everything was going to be fine and dandy. Such a doctor would have to be either lying or stupid. So pay no heed to the rantings of any politician; their natterings are nothing but verbal garbage, poisoning the souls of hopeful fools exactly like the other politicians who once dominated the stage, basked in the spotlight, and did what they could, or didn't do what they could, but did what they did to get the rest of us into this terrible spot form which there is no escape.

Garbage! Smog! Shit! Filth! This is the legacy of the western world to whatever chipmunks, field mice, and butterflies that might still remain when The Great Hush shall fall over the world.

What a sight it will be when all the alligators come crawling out of the sewers and head back to Okefinokee Swamp. For them too the hayride will be over. Will they all be blind from having lived too long in the dark? We are; why should they have it any better!

My, oh my, won't they be big and fat though! Oh, they eat what I told you they eat all right, make no mistake about it. What did you think happened to an aborted baby. Did you think they were put in a little white casket and driven to the cemetery in a Cadillac hearse and covered with a blanket of carnations while Father Flanagan recited the twenty-second Psalm and mommy and daddy sobbed softly?

Like HELL! The fetus, heart still beating or not, is thrown into the BTR machine--The Bulk Tissue Reducer--and slash-cut-spin-grind go the stainless steel blades. A high-pitched whine, not unlike that of a kitchen blender, fills the room and in a matter of seconds everything is reduced to a thick, sweet-smelling syrup. Yes, the BTR is quite the handy gadget. Amputated arms and legs go in there, gall bladders, appendices, cancerous breasts, goiters, lungs, bones, and babies by the ton. Whir-r-r, quiver, whine . . . and don't those razor-sharp blades do a marvelous job! Eyeballs, earlobes, ovaries, lashes, lips, fingernails, all ground down to a grainy jello in a handful of heartbeats. Goodbye, Einstein. Goodbye, Mohammed. Goodbye, Baruch, Lincoln, Shakespeare. Bye-bye, Baby Jesus. After all, alligators got to live too, don't they.

And there goes mother swinging down the sidewalk. What! back on her feet already? Certainly! life goes on, doesn't it. Doesn't it? See Jane run. See Jane go on with her career: Executive Vice-President, Photo Lay-Out, Hustler, Inc. Twenty-eight Big Ones per annum. Wow! Thursday night she'll have to put on her leather undies and tell her NOW group all about it.

* * *

*Ladies and Gentlemen, I know that many of you have been in prison. I think that's wonderful. It's lucky for you that you know what The Man is like. Not what he should be, and not what he pretends to be, but what he really, truly is. He's a mean, savage son-of-a bitch, boys, and I hope to shit in your mess kit if I'm lying. Sure, you maybe paid a hell of a price to find this out, but you did learn a very important lesson and that's all that matters. You've got a stupendous advantage over these hairpins that maintain man is something made in the image and likeness of God. Because you and I know better. There's no call for us to worry about what man should be or can be; we deal exclusively with what is, with reality.

Incidentally, people, these boxes of ribs and this beer is for anyone to help themselves. If anybody knows where we can get a better mess of ribs, just let us know and we'll get some. Since Skip's went out of business it's hard to find good ribs anymore.

But I'm asking if you'll throw the bones and the cans in the trash baskets and try to keep this place half-way neat because I don't want to forfeit our deposit. I'm sure you understand.

Yes, prisons fulfill a number of functions besides the one for which they are designed. The main thing wrong is that, for the most part, the wrong people are doing time. Now, you and I both know that there are some really bad dudes going time; guys like Manson and Speck and T. Eugene Thompson, but most of the jokers at Graystone College are nothing but social misfits. Out of about eleven hundred cats at Stillwater right now, a good three hundred of them are there for non-support, and, my God! you could hardly call people like this desperados.

Another three hundred are there for hanging paper. Almost all these guys are alcoholics. They'll go out drinking, go broke, and write a bad check. Yes, they're a pain in the ass and, yes, what they do is stealing, but still I don't feel they belong in a prison cell for five, six, or seven years for doing it.

The point is that the wrong people are

in prison, or the right people are there for too long a time, or at least it seems that way. Prisons are populated only with dummies, guys that aren't smart enough, or clever enough, or rich enough, to do what they want to do and get away with it.

What would really be neat would be to lock up some of these assholes who truly deserve to be punished. Like, how about some of these big oil company executives. Don't they deserve a little something for the obscene way they bleed the American public. And how about those cocksuckers at General Motors who OKd production of the Corvair when they knew its design was faulty and that thousands of trusting buyers were going to be killed or maimed for life by the shitty thing.

Or how about these motherfuckers at Amway, still peddling their alfalfa-watercress-parsley pills. Uncle Sam tried for four years to put these turds in prison but all that was gained was that the slippery bastards had to stop claiming their Nutrilite garbage would cure twenty-seven diseases, including athletes foot and cancer. These weasels are still in business, still cheating people right and left and teaching their disciples, in turn, how to cheat other people. They're the biggest parasites in America; they create nothing, they only exploit the system and the greed of the little materialists who can't see the forest for the trees.

Yes, these are certainly, beyond any doubt, the people who should be stripped naked, flogged, and shut up in a steel cage--not the ridiculous little teen-age joyriders, the petty burglars, and the pitiful collection of losers that presently make up the bulk of America's prison population.

But that's the way it is, boys, and nothing much is ever going to change. Neither you nor I can do much about the social order because, one, they are many and we are few. And, two, they are organized and very strong. And, three, there isn't time enough anymore. This country is like an out-of-control race car just before she hits the wall. The time to do something was way back there on the curve when things first went wrong. Not now. The wall is six inches away; there's no time.

Believe me, people, neither you nor I, nor one of us here in this room will ever dance in the sunshine again. Because for America it's all over. Her days are numbered and that's a fact. But, by God, we certainly are going to go out in style, that much I guarantee you. You and I are going to see things never before seen by man. In the days of darkness and terror we shall be riding high. For we, the members of C.O.B.R.A., have all that it takes to florish and prosper when panic sweeps the streets and screams rent the night and mass confusion reigns and the thunder of death resounds across the land.

Come to our next meeting next Friday night at seven-thirty and I will continue.

Thank you.

* * *

The Caterpillar operator showed up just after dawn and knocked on the farmhouse door while Zeff and Eckman were still asleep. Eckman got dressed quickly and went outside to show the fellow where he had staked out an area about fifty feet south of the house.

"I want the bottom of the trench fifteen feet below ground level and I want it flat on the bottom for about twenty-five feet. Don't make the incline and decline angles too steep or I won't be able to drive in and get out; I'm going to pull a big fuel tank in there and bury it."

The operator, who looked too young to know how to run a Caterpillar, was dressed in faded Levis and wore a Minnesota Twins baseball cap. He stood looking over the situation, shifting the wad of chewing tobacco in his cheek and spitting thoughtfully. "Any pipes?" he asked laconically, "Gas, water, sewer?"

"Nothing at all," Eckman told him. He had no idea if there were or not.

"Telephone cable?"

"No, we don't have a telephone."

The kid thought this over. "OK, I'll

have right at it. Lowboy's coming for me at eleven. Got another job." Still spitting, he walked over to the D-4, which had been sitting there over a week, climbed up, and started it. Eckman watched him maneuver it around into position for the first cut and then went back inside and made coffee.

Zeff was awake now. "Christ in heaven," he muttered, "do I have to put up with that all day? Who is it, your grave-digger?"

"Yeah, he finally got here. It won't take him long. Want some coffee, Charlie?"

Less than twenty minutes later, Zeff announced he was going to walk into town. The roaring and clanking of the machine got on his nerves, he said. He'd hang around town, maybe go down to the bowling alley for awhile, and walk back sometime this afternoon.

After he left, Eckman sat by the kitchen window drinking his warm coffee and thinking. First thing tomorrow he'd go into Minneapolis and find a trailer for sale. Getting someone to haul it out here was going to be a nuisance but he'd figure something out later. The main thing was to get the thing underground and the ground leveled off again as soon as possible. With a little luck this could all be done in a few days, he thought.

Some time later, casting about for something to do, Eckman's eye fell upon the footlocker containing Zeff's manuscripts. He went over and opened it and began going through them. Each manuscript was in a plain manila filing folder with the name of the book printed on it in red block letters. Most of them were contemporary action novels but there were also westerns, mysteries, a collection of short stories, and even a thin folder of sonnets.

Eckman selected a thick folder of short stories, opened it at random, and began reading a short-short called, "The Boy Who Used His Head":

Long ago when the world was young, there lived a little boy in the far away mountains of Gemaria. His name was Fazio Fox and he had the most ugly face of any boy in the entire world. His eyes were a dull yellow color. His cheeks were gray and spotted with terrible red blisters. His nose was long and pointed and bent way over to one side. His mouth was crooked and his pointed teeth grew this way and that in such a fashion that all who looked at him were filled with fear. Poor, ugly Fazio Fox; what a horrible face he had.

Fazio Fox made his living by playing the drum. Rum-dum, rum-dum-dum; all day he marched through the streets playing his drum so the people would throw him pennies. Sometimes he would make twelve or fourteen cents in a day but so ugly was his face that many people would run the other way when they saw him coming.

As Fazio Fox got older and uglier, more and more people would run the other way when they saw him coming and there were fewer and fewer pennies tossed to him. Finally the day came when not one single penny came his way. Rum-dum, rum-dum, rum-rum-rum-dee-dum; all through the heat of the day F.F. played his drum but when night fell there was not a single penny in his pocket.

"I'll have no supper tonight," Fazio Fox told himself sadly, "for I have no money. I want an egg, a piece of cheese, two hot biscuits, a bowl of milk, and a jar of pudding. But it takes money to buy these things and when there is no money there can be no supper. It is my ugly face that is causing all this trouble. It is my ugly face which makes people run away when they see me coming."

So Fazio Fox sat down on his drum and tried to think of what to do. And then suddenly he knew what to do. Quick as a flash he jumped up from his drum and ran down to the city dump. There in the dump he picked up pieces of paper, bits of rags, and little cans of paint. And that night Fazio Fox went to work making the mask that he was to wear for the rest of his days.

The next morning the job was done. Fazio put on the mask and tied it in place with a big white strap which went around the back of his head. Then, taking his drum, he went out into the streets and began beating on it just as he had always done. Rum-dum, rum-dum-dum.

"Oh, look!" the people cried, "look at that darling drummer boy with the ugly mask. Only a beautiful boy would dare wear such a mask; come, let us reward him." And the nickels and dimes rained down upon Fazio Fox till his pockets bulged with coins.

For the people loved that mask. It had gray cheeks, a long bent nose, a crooked mouth, and pointed teeth. But, after all, as anyone could see, it was only a mask. And Fazio Fox was the only person in the world who knew that the mask was exactly the same as the face it hid.

And he ate big suppers for the rest of his life.

* * *

Eckman was amused. Pensive, he sat there for a moment. Then, just as he was about to replace all the manuscripts, he noticed a package wrapped in red tissue paper at the very bottom of the footlocker. Curious, he unwrapped it and saw that it was another manuscript. Like the others, it had its title printed on the folder: "A Songbird at Sundown." Wondering why this particular manuscript had been specially wrapped, Eckman carried it to his bunk, lay down, and began reading:

Autant d'hommes, autant d'avis; so many men, so many minds. But how similar the rich man poor man beggar man thief, how alike their soft screams. Give me, Lord, a rainproof roof and a hot supper, a job to do, a child to rear, some health hope help, a warm quilt for the final chills, and love. Please! some love.

I had that love. From September of 1937 up to the last year of the Korean War I loved, lived with, and was loved by, a woman so exquisitely satisfying that I can never, even when I shiver beneath the useless warmth of my quilt,--I can never envy the young. For I had my youth and I had my love. If I cheated and lied to get it, if I broke with convention to enjoy it, if I fought God to keep it, the fact remains that I hurt no one and so whose concern is it but my own.

A psychiatrist who examined me in 1953 wanted to write the story of Helen Michelle and me but I would not permit him. To spell out every sigh and secret of such a delicate, intense relationship would be outrageous tampering with the sacred. The fact that Helen did not exist in any earthly sense meant nothing to me. "She is mine," I told the doctor, "She is what I prayed for and got and she is why I keep fighting and keep living." When he told me my love would not last I laughed in his face. He was right, of course, but even today I have no regrets for those eighteen years. So many men, so many minds, so many means to an end!

My name is Jamaica Valentine and I was born at the Surfrider Hotel in Kingston on November 12, 1915. My father was a successful textile manufacturer and importer. Because he was abroad so much of the time though, I hardly knew him and when he was killed in one of the student demonstrations in Hong Kong, I do not remember feeling very sad. That was in 1925, I believe, for I was in Fifth Grade.

My mother took me to England for the seven months it took for our Winston plant to straighten itself out but, since none of this is important, it is enough to say that we—my mother and I—eventually settled in San Francisco and began a life of very modest means indeed.

Our careless Jamaican holiday was over now and the rum-soaked sugar sticks were gone forever. Mother began work in the gift-wrapping department at I. Magnin and I was put in a public school out on Potrero.

* * *

Totally absorbed, Eckman kept reading Zeff's book. Nearly three hours passed before a sudden silence jolted him loose and he realized the Caterpillar had stopped running.

Going outside, he saw that the job was not only completed but the machine had already been trucked away. The operator was leaning against his van studying a road map.

"Nice job," Eckman told him, looking down into the hole. He had not expected it to be so big.

"Think that'll do yuh?" the driver said.

"Sure. It's fine. Want me to sign something?"

The driver produced a work sheet, extended it to Eckman, then folded it and got into his van. "See you around," he said. Then he was gone.

Eckman went back inside and continued reading. As the story went on, he found himself pausing now from time to time and looking away from the pages, wondering what it was that was puzzling him. He knew now that he had seriously underestimated Zeff's skill as a writer; the guy was very, very good. Parts of the book seemed astonishingly believable. They rang so true that Eckman found it difficult deciding which parts were the creation of Zeff's imagination and which parts were lifted directly from the poor little guy's life. The main character was a man who called himself Valen. This guy was, among other things, a demolitions expert. He tried and failed at many things and whenever he was defeated in some way, he would research the pattern of living of the person who had wronged him and then plant a bomb along that person's path, intending to kill him. As life handed him one disappointment after another, he eventually began spending all his time planting these deadly devices and by the time he was fifty-three years old he had a hundred and seventeen of them all ready and waiting. Oddly, he never actually detonated any of them. Simply knowing he could kill someone he hated any time he chose gave him all the satisfaction he needed to keep going.

Valen lived in Minneapolis and had these bombs buried all over the city and all around the suburbs. Usually he would plant them when a supermarket or office building or sidewalk was being constructed or was under repair. Any construction project caught his eye and if the location was suitable he would approach it after dark and incorporate his carefully protected bomb right into the structure.

Almost all of them had the same type of fuse. Valen used spring-loaded contacts ingeniously held open by a thin-walled vial of sulfuric acid which, when broken, released the acid into a lead tube, creating an electrical charge of sufficient power to trigger the bomb. The vial was broken sonically by any device held against the wall, ground, or roadway which transmitted the ultra-high sound at the correct frequency. It was a marvelously simple and efficient fuse, impervious to time and, because of the way it was sealed, all the elements. Tests conducted by Valen proved it worked perfectly, even when buried behind as much as three feet of concrete.

"God in heaven," Eckman exclaimed aloud, "that damn Zeff has got one hell of an imagination. Jesus H. Christ!"

At four o'clock, when Zeff got back, Eckman was just finishing, "A Songbird at Sundown."

Zeff stopped dead in his tracks in the doorway and looked first at the red tissue paper on the kitchen table and then at Eckman. "Who the fuck said you could read that book," he shouted, his face livid; "I don't want you prowling around in my stuff. Put that back where you got it."

Eckman, stunned, made no move as Zeff snatched the manuscript from him and began rewrapping it in the tissue. "This book is private; I poured my guts into it and I don't want anybody looking at it."

"Then why even bother writing it," Eckman asked. "If you just write for yourself then you must be some kind of a nut." He began to get angry. His face flushed slightly and he raised his voice. "And not only that, but you *told* me I could read your books. In fact I read at least two of them when you were right here."

"Not this one," Zeff insisted, "I never said you could read this one. It's personal;

158

that's why I had it wrapped up." He had calmed down and now, after a silence, he turned around and faced Eckman. "Well, as long as you read it, what did you think?"

Eckman never hesitated. "I think it's the best damn thing you ever wrote," he said fervently. "I think you could easily have it published and make yourself a bundle. It comes across authentic as hell. How do you dream that shit up anyway!"

Zeff had rewrapped the manuscript now and placed it back in the footlocker. When he spoke the words came slowly. He stared at the fingernails of his half-closed hand and his voice was hardly more than a whisper. "I didn't dream that one up, buddy. The damn thing is true. It's the story of my life. That's why I don't like anybody to read it."

"Bullshit!" Eckman exclaimed. "It can't be true. You weren't born in Jamaica. You've never even been near the place. And your old man was no big-shot textile manufacturer, he was a streetcar conductor in Wichita-
-you told me so yourself, more than once."

"Oh, that part is fiction," Zeff said quickly; "that was just frosting on the cake. I jazzed it up a little to give the reader a little treat. But the main part of the book, the part about all my bombs, is true. Every word of it. And I ought to know; I'm Valen."

Donald Eckman, speechless, stared at

his old friend. Neither man spoke for a long time. Eckman's mind raced back over the years, recalling what he could remember of Charlie Zeff's life and matching the bits and pieces against events in the book. Zeff *had* been involved in an unhappy marriage, he *had* lost a number of very good jobs, he *had* been handed a few raw deals. And there was no doubt about his being a master explosives technician. Still . . .

"Did you actually plant all those bombs, Charlie? No bullshit now, did you really?"

"Yes, Don, I really did. Just exactly like it says in the book. In fact, the book tells exactly where I put every single one of them. Some of them have been there since '54 and I could detonate them right today if I wanted to."

"I wonder how many would still go off after all this time," Eckman said.

"They all would," Zeff replied blandly. "Remember, I was trained in this. I've got them in air-tight vacuum pouches and some of them use Dupont plastique with no known life limitation."

Eckman was thinking of what he had just read. "And do you really have some of them built right into a freeway?"

"I've got seven or eight of them buried in the concrete of every freeway in the metropolitan area. They're all tuned for different frequencies but the numbers in the book are the right ones. That's another reason I keep the book under wraps; it's the only record I have."

Now Eckman had a thousand questions. How powerful was each bomb? Were there actually two of them in the new Federal Courthouse? Could they be detected electronically? Why had Zeff placed one at the main gate of every cemetery? And, most of all, why hadn't he ever detonated one!"

"Just knowing I *could* was enough for me, Don. It gave me a sense of power knowing that someone I hated was alive and healthy only because I permitted him to be. It was almost like being God.

"I never really wanted to hurt anyone, and in fact I never did. Then, as I got older I got more mellow and I decided to write it all down and see what kind of a story it would make. I never would have done that if I hadn't abandoned the idea of actually killing with the damn things, but at the same time, I don't want just anybody reading the book."

"It's one hell of a book, all right," Eckman said. "Not many people would pick a method of revenge that involved twenty or thirty years of waiting."

"There are all kinds of people with what you might call a defective conception of time," Zeff told him. "They can't distinguish the difference between two months and five years and what seems like a lifetime to most people is only ten minutes to them. That's the way Valen is."

"But you said you're Valen!"

"I was, but I'm not any more, Don. And that's a fact!"

Late that night the pain awoke Eckman from a fitful sleep and he coughed weakly. He thought of Zeff's bombs buried and waiting all over the city and silently he cursed every cigarette he had ever smoked. A fine sweat covered his body before the pain subsided this time and he thought, oh, what I could have done if I'd known about those bombs ten years ago. If only, if only, if only . . .

He coughed softly till nearly four. Then he slept.

* * *

March came in like a lion. Overnight the false spring faded and the north wind sprang to life, howling under the eaves, rattling the windows, and dumping six inches of snow on the sullen, winter-weary midwest. I flew to Ottawa on Air Canada and picked up a twenty-ounce cannister of IVG-5 crystals which I knew had been stashed there since 1968 with an exiled member of the IRA, a man currently sought in both Ulster and the Republic of Ireland for terrorist killings in Belfast, Dun Laoghaire, and Liverpool. This poison was absolutely and beyond any doubt the most powerful, deadly substance on earth. It was developed in the 'Fifties by a dissident faction of young Jewish militants. Chemically formulated in France, it was tested and perfected at the University of Vienna and finally manufactured, ironically, in Dusseldorf. It was intended to be introduced into the German water supply as an act of retribution for the crimes committed against Jews by the German people and so potent was IVG-5 that it was conservatively estimated seventy-eight percent of all the people in Germany could be killed within eighteen hours. When the final plan was submitted to the Knesset, however, it was, after lengthy examination and discussion, absolutely and irrevocably disapproved by the council and both the existing poison and the formula for it were ordered destroyed. I learned all this from the IRA man, although how this one batch of the stuff ever got into Canada, or for what reason, was something he never told me, nor did I ask.

I paid for it with twenty-one Krugerrands, which was the price designated, and I sat at the table sipping the bottle of Carling's Black Label ale he had offered me and wondering if I had been snookered. Because of course I had no way of knowing for sure at this time whether or not the sealed glass bottle packed inside the black and yellow can really contained IVG-5 as represented.

But it didn't take me long to find out. Back in Minneapolis, the very next day, I bought two white mice and, wearing rubber gloves and a surgical mask as I had been warned to, mixed a bit of the coarse, gray and white crystals with a teaspoonful of water and then used a plastic soda straw to place a single drop on the head of one mouse, between his ears. I set down the straw and then peered at the creature closely, wanting to see if it affected him and how soon. For a full fifteen seconds I watched him until I suddenly realized he was neither moving nor even blinking his eyes. I nudged him with my finger and he rolled over. Only then did it dawn on me he was dead. Astonished, I picked up the other mouse and it was squeaking and struggling when, as a variation, I put one drop on the tip of its nose. Instantly, as fast as the click of a switch turns off a lamp, the mouse was dead.

I lit a cigarette and sat there thinking for maybe five minutes. Later, I decided, I would try it on a larger animal, a cat or a dog. But for now I screwed the glass cap back on the bottle and placed it on the top shelf of the kitchen cupboard. I had other things to think about.

* * *

By St. Patrick's Day all the snow was gone. The temperature climbed into the 'fifties and a few kites and songbirds appeared. Spring at last was here. One morning I got up early and took a long walk around the loop. At seven-thirty I found myself standing on a bridge over 35W watching the endless line of cars and trucks coming into town. This was something I had done many times before, watch the lemmings. My God, I thought, just look at all those fucking morons. They jump in their seven thousand dollar piece of chrome-plated Detroit tin and then, nerves taut, battle their way grimly down the freeway, cursing each other, cutting in and out, tromping down now on the gas and now on the brake—and for what? To get downtown at their stupid, asinine, pointless, ridiculous job in order to make enough money to pay for the car that got them there!

But today I didn't linger and watch them as long as I usually did. I was weary of this game now as I was weary of all the little games I had played for so many years. Never once, ever, had I even remotely suspected that days like these had always been awaiting me. I thought that things would never change, and maybe they hadn't, but I changed and my values changed and all my wishes and dreams changed. I had managed to survive until now I was in that stage of life where I was not only aware of my mortality, but also exquisitely conscious of my own frailty and vulnerability. For me there would be no more springs. How easy it was to say yet how odd to know. Did I ever think the day would come when I would grow tired of the world; when, of my own volition I would say, "Enough!"?

Yet that was the choice I had made and having made it, even as I breathed a sigh of relief, there was a certain quiet reflection, a shadow of childlike wonder at what death was really like. Surely it was the ultimate adventure. Billions of others had gone before me and now they knew. And soon I would know. Very soon. Before the pumpkins ripened I would know why the dead, they are so quiet.

Would my life have been radically different if I had been loved as a child? Certainly! And yet I was glad I had never loved or been loved; I was grateful for the good fortune to have been exempted from all such foolishness. For I never believed, not for an instant, that there really is any such thing on this earth as love. How could I believe in something I had never seen or experienced. What I did see palmed off as love was nothing but people using people, consciously or otherwise, for their own comfort or gratification. Love promises that which only God can deliver, something which absolutely does not exist in this sad place called earth. Only the illusion exists and I was weary of illusions.

Was there a chance I might live to regret what I was about to do? Yes, there definitely was such a chance because once I took such a drastic step I knew I could not be the same person I was today. Maybe I'd be satisfied or may I'd be ashamed. But if indeed I found myself unhappy from the act, then I would console myself with the fact that the decisions I'd made were based upon the best information I had at the time I made them and so, with this to sustain me, I knew I would not cringe or crumble. All learning involves movement of some kind and the score of any lifetime spent selecting solutions to problems is bound to reveal quite a number of errors. After all, no one's perfect; not even me.

* * *

Purely by coincidence, Nancy was alone at the apartment the afternoon that Vince Savanna burst in with the news of Zeff and Eckman and the buried trailer at Cecil Cohen's farm. He was highly excited. "Nancy, I swear to God, it's the damnest thing I ever saw. No shit! I mean these are some really strung-out cats. They actually did this! Maybe they live in a world of their own but, by God, at least they *do* things. Listen to this tape I have here of Eckman talking. Just listen to the guy and then tell me what you think." Savanna plugged in the small Panasonic which, along with one cassette, Zeff had let him borrow. The tape began playing at once. It was Eckman giving his angry opinion of crooked cops, homosexuals, Japanese toys, Mormons, and bartenders.

Nancy was fascinated. She sat on the edge of the couch, hands folded in her lap, and listened intently until the machine clicked off a full thirty minutes later. Then she burst into laughter. "This guy is great," she said; "who is he anyway? He sounds exactly like Chris! Boy! wait'll Chris hears this; those two ought to get together, they're on the same wave length!"

Then Nancy wanted to hear all about the buried trailer and Savanna told her what he had learned in the half day he had spent on the farm. "Nancy, it's the neatest thing you ever saw; it's slicker than hot leopard shit. This Eckman bought a twenty-eight foot New Moon and dragged it into this hole he'd dug and then wrapped it with a plastic haystack cover. He dug a trench around the base of it, then poured concrete into the trench and stuck steel fenceposts into the concrete eight inches apart. Then he laid boiler plate over the top and used a tractor with a front-end loader to fill everything in. He's got five feet of dirt covering the whole works. It's waterproof and with all those steel posts around it he claims it's an escape-proof prison--and I believe him!"

Nancy tried to picture it in her mind. "How do you get into it," she asked.

"You go down a ladder, straight down,

and then he's got a steel door you have to unbolt before you can open the trailer door."

"A home-made prison," Nancy mused. "Why did he do it? Who are the prisoners going to be?"

"He wouldn't say," Savanna replied. "He said they were just assholes he knew, people who deserved it. And I almost forgot to tell you, you ought to see how you get into the place. To get to the top of the ladder you have to lift a wooden hatch that he built to look exactly like a little pile of split stove wood. This pile is on the edge of a three or four cord stack of wood and it looks natural as hell. There's no way you'd ever think it was anything except part of the woodpile out there in the yard."

Nancy said, "A person would suffocate."

"Oh, no," Savanna told her. "He's got a pipe and a blower and a couple of exhaust vents. He even ran a power cord in so there's a few lights. And he's got the toilet running into an old hot water heater he punched full of holes and dropped in a hole underneath the trailer. I tell you, the guy thought of everything; you've got to give him credit."

Nancy said she wanted to go out and see the setup for herself.

"Eckman doesn't want anyone coming out there right now," Savanna said, "He'll be at our next meeting, or at least he said he would be, but he told me flat out he wants no one around the place. You can talk to him yourself next Friday. I told him where to come and I could tell he was interested."

"How come he trusts you so much then," Nancy asked. "He doesn't even know you."

"We're both cons. We speak the same lingo. We never did time in the same joint but that doesn't make any difference; they're all the same."

"How about this guy, Zeff; "what's he like?"

"He seemed pretty quiet. He's just a little guy, kind of bookish. I really didn't talk much with him. He thinks Eckman is crazier than hell but he likes him and he thinks Eckman's private prison is very amusing. He claims he's going to write a book about it."

"He's a writer?"

"Yeah, that's what I understand."

Again Nancy laughed. "Boy! I can't wait till Chris gets a load of this. I can see where it might tie in with some of our C.O.B.R.A. plans very, very nicely!"

* * *

As far as I could determine, the Minneapolis waterworks had no security system whatsoever. Located just north of town on the Mississippi River, the plant sprawled over forty park-like acres and it's only defense against people like me appeared to be a common chain link fence. There were no armed guards, no dogs, and no sign of any electronic surveillance. I was almost appalled at realizing its vulnerability.

Merely for the asking, I was given a detailed schematic of the entire system. It showed all the buildings and explained their function, and all the pipelines were carefully drawn in. This was handed me on a public tour of the place. I made only a single phone call to be included on this tour and none of us were questioned, photographed, or fingerprinted.

I had already decided not to introduce the IVG-5 at the plant itself because I thought they might have sensing devices built into the system which might detect it and shut off the flow of water into the city. But I was glad to get a copy of the pipeline layout because it saved me a lot of time and trouble digging through old documents at both the City Engineer's office and the public library.

I ordered a small 220-volt override pump from a company in Gary, Indiana, thinking I could tear it apart and redesign it to run on compressed air. After it came and I'd examined it however, I realized that I lacked the know-how to do this, to say nothing of the machine tools, so I chucked the whole idea. Then, in my very next move, I found myself on the right track. At a toy store, I bought a number of different makes of radio-controlled toy cars. I removed their guts and screwed around until I had devised a linkage which, upon receiving the correct radio signal, would move to plunge a pin into a small cylinder of seltzer-bottle CO_2 gas. This cylinder was threaded into a can containing the IVG-5 and the can was adapted with a nipple about the size of a tire valve, only longer, and it screwed down into the water pipe, which of course I had to drill and tap. Thus, when I was done, I had merely to press a button on my cigar-box-size transmitter and the CO_2 cylinder would be punctured and the force of the highly-compressed gas would blast the poison past a little seventy-seven cent spring-loaded ball valve directly into the flow of water.

Working alone, always in the early morning hours, I attached thirteen cans of poison to all the main water pipes over a period of nine days. Almost all of the pipes were cast iron and easy to drill but I used diamond drills anyway, for speed, and I always carried several spares. To avoid drilling into a pipe that was under pressure, I picked up a Japanese gauge which, when fastened to the pipe by a suction connector, was supposed to indicate how much pressure the pipe was under. How accurate this gauge was I do not know but all of my drilling was uneventful and I never got wet.

Before my device could be operative it

was necessary to attach a short antenna but rather than have someone stumble across this antenna, or have some hobbyist accidently trigger the thing, I left the antenna off for the time being. I twisted wire-knits onto the antenna wire and buried the end of it just under the ground, marking its location carefully in a notepad I carried.

This project completed, I moved on to the next.

* * *

Evasion and denial were never my favorite defense mechanisms. Thus, I saw clearly that matters were getting out of hand at C.O.B.R.A. long before the shit hit the fan. Two things, I think, led to the trouble. First, I never had any training, or any ability, or any real interest, in organization. It's just not my bag. The detailed planning, the myriad of severely prosiac stepstones, the pure and simple mathematics of it, bores the piss out of me. I mean, if I were possessed, yes! if I were possessed of the analytical type brain I would have been a CPA, or I would have taken a Ph.D. in optics and gone to work designing circuitry for Matsushita Electric, or I might have taken up music. But I'm the intuitive type. I shoot from the hip and play it by ear and let the little voice in the back of my head give the orders.

Sometimes I got fooled. Sometimes the little voice steers me wrong. Especially when I'm drinking. Why in the name of Sweet Baby Jesus I started drinking at such a critical moment is something I do not know. Was it because I was happy, flush with success, or was it maybe to throw ice water on the red-hot demons that were driving me. Certainly I knew that alcohol was a depressant and that my ass would be buttermilk for at least three days following a good bender--yet I did it anyway; knowingly, willingly, wrongfully, and stupidly.

The next thing I knew was that somebody who called themself "Angel Lady" had distributed something like four hundred T-shirts around town, in fact sold them for nine dollars each, on which was printed a truly ferocious looking cobra with a flattened hood and an impressively swollen head. The snake, which rose out of its own coils was red. Underneath, in black and yellow letters, was printed C.O.B.R.A.

Overnight these T-shirts became a cult sensation. The person who dreamed up the whole idea, a black woman from the northside, sold, as I say, four hundred of them in three weeks. Channel 11 did a spot special on them and, my God, they were everywhere. High school kids were wearing them, Hennepin Avenue pimps were wearing them; even joggers! Since we had less than three hundred real members of C.O.B.R.A. at this time, I knew we had created a fanciful game and so, without attempting to direct or plan or reinforce or anticipate anything, but merely as an exercise, I told Nancy that I wanted to say something to the black dude who had told the wrong person--or perhaps the right person-- that he was thinking of knocking off a bank in south Minneapolis while wearing a cobra shirt.

He got in touch with me right away and within two hours we met at a bar on East Hennepin, not far from DeLaSalle High School. I liked the man right from the start. He was younger than he should have been but he knew the difference between Tuesday and Chicago. I laid it on him right off that I didn't have time for no shucking and jivin' and I asked him how much he figured he could grab in a oneshot hustle. When he said six or seven I pulled a banded pack of hundreds out of my boot and slapped them on the table under his nose.

"Here's ten biggies right here, I told him. "Do it my way, exactly my way, and I'll give this to you tomorrow night, same time, same station, if you give me half of everything you get."

His lids narrowed. He looked at the pack of hundred dollar bills, picked them up, fanned them and then drilled me with his dark brown eyes. Finally he said he would listen.

At two-thirty the next afternoon it was on all the news. A masked bandit, wearing a C.O.B.R.A. shirt, had robbed a Twin City Federal branch of thirty-four thousand dollars. There were no leads.

He met me at sundown and gave me seven thousand dollars, exactly what he owed me. This time he wasn't quite so tough as he'd been the day before. "How you do that," he asked.

"Did you walk in the door at exactly 2:05," I asked.

"Yes."

"Did you walk calmly to all three tellers and keep your voice natural and pleasant?"

"Yes."

"Did you leave the bank at exactly 2:08 and walk, don't run, like I told you?"

"I did. Yes, yes."

"Then did you calmly drive to 42nd Street and park by the black Mustang at the drive-in and were the keys in the ignition like I said they would be!"

Now my compotator could only stare at me.

"You're very bold," I told him, "and you're also a bit too trusting. But this time you trusted the right cat. I told you yesterday I'd have the man running in circles, and I did, but never mind how I did it. Let's just say I messed up their communications and I intend to do it again too; anytime I want." I told the dude to hang loose; that I might have another deal for him later. Then I made it.

I was jubilant. Not because I'd make seven easy bills but because more than ever now I was starting to glow with the accumulation of evidence that no one had a snowball's chance against me.

The night-fighter had driven cool as a breeze down Nicollet Ave. in broad daylight with no hassle from the heat because I had planted five cheap tape-recorders on five roof tops. All were timed to start playing at 2:05. Endless-loop tapes then spat out nonsense street numbers, code calls, curse words, letters, and the names of actual police officers, flooding the four law enforcement agency frequencies with such a conglomeration of senseless static that, in effect, no cop in Minneapolis knew what was happening. A little linear amplification boosted the strength of my transmissions, adding to the confusion, and by the time the tapes clicked off my jungle-bunny was in the Mustang. I was real proud of the guy for wearing our shirt; the closed-circuit cameras in the bank picked it up real nice. C.O.B.R.A. was in the news and on the move!

Secretly however, I was troubled by the disorganized, unruly mob of riffraff. I knew I was not their leader, not really, and I started wondering if the scumbags might eventually prove to be more trouble than they were worth.

* * *

It was several days after this caper that Vince Savanna and I finally met face to face for the first time. We met in a White Castle on Lake Street and he repeated to me what he had told Nancy about Eckman and the farm. He studied me carefully, tilting his head and examining my every feature. At first this annoyed me but I suppose it was only natural that he should be curious. He seemed much more restrained and less animated than Nancy had led me to expect but perhaps that was merely the effect I had upon him.

Nancy had been right when she said he was an extremely good-looking man. Indeed he was. He was also much bigger than I'd thought, well over six feet tall, and I was somehow surprised to see him so neatly groomed.

But I can't say that we hit it off too well, at least at the beginning. No sooner did we sit down with our coffee than he asked why Janski, Patman, and Good had been returned to prison. I didn't feel like informing him that this was part of the arrangement. "Don't ask me," I said with a shrug, "Maybe they couldn't stay sober; who knows."

"It just seems like a dirty way of playing around with a guy," Savanna said sulkily. I didn't like this attitude of his but I decided to remain silent.

Next he wanted to know who Martin Fox and George Gannon were. "They have nothing to do with us," I answered truthfully; "they're just people I hired to do one specific job. You won't ever see either of them again."

Savanna thought this over. "Then who sends me my money every week?"

I saw no reason to tell him it was I. "What difference does it make," I said calmly. "As long as you do your job you've got no problems."

We made arrangements to drive to Cecil Cohen's farm the next morning. As I walked out I could feel him staring after me. I had to admit there was something about Vincent Savanna that made me uncomfortable.

* * *

It was a gray and gloomy Monday morning in early April when the three of us, Savanna, Nancy, and myself, set out on the ninety minute drive to the farm. Nancy had insisted upon coming along and she sat between Savanna and me, on the motor cover of the old Ford van Savanna had brought. None of us felt very cheerful and there was very little conversation.

In spite of what the calendar said, it still was not so much early spring as it was late winter. Patches of sooty snow still covered most of the fields and the strands of barren, leafless timber only added to the desolate scene of grimy, weather-beaten farm buildings, scruffy, mud-caked cattle, and the few lonely people bending grimly into a sharp, unfriendly wind.

At Waverly, where we stopped for coffee, I bought a case of beer and a two-liter jug of vodka. Then I walked to the super-market and bought a barbequed chicken, still hot from the rotissiere. I thought someone might be getting hungry before we headed back.

When we finally got to the farm, I found myself looking for the woodpile, and then staring at it, even as we drove down the dirt road leading from the blacktop to the house. I tried to guess which small stack of log ends covered the entrance to the trailer. But there was no way to tell. It looked simply like an ordinary, if rather carelessly stacked supply of firewood.

Suddenly, when we were almost to the house, there was a tremendous explosion in the plowed field just off the road to our left. White smoke filled the air and big clods of dirt thudded down on the van. Savanna, too startled to curse, slammed on the brakes and both he and I opened our doors to leap out. Almost at once there was another blast, this one on my side, and again smoke and dirt shot up, spattering the windshield and us with lumps of mud. It was Korea all over again.

"Take cover," I shouted, but just as I was to dive under the van I saw Zeff and Eckman appear on the porch of the farmhouse. Both were laughing.

"Advance and be recognized," one of them yelled as both of them walked toward us. For some reason or other I found myself laughing also, although I wasn't sure why.

The smaller of the two men, who turned out to be Zeff, was shaking hands with Savanna now. "Hi, Vince," he said, "how do you like our security setup!"

"Christ, man," Savanna replied, "you want to kill somebody? You guys nuts!"

"Oh, they won't hurt you," Zeff said, "it's just ammonium nitrate to shake up unwanted visitors." He looked at me and Nancy, who was still in the truck. "These your friends you were telling me about?"

Savanna introduced us and we all went into the kitchen of the farmhouse. Nancy couldn't wait to be shown the trailer. "OK," Eckman said, "but when you get back to town don't be spreading it all over the place because I don't want everybody and his brother knowing about it."

Once we were down in the trailer, I found it to be pretty much as Savanna had described it and, although I looked about with interest, I found nothing particularly fascinating about it and I was ready to go topside again after about five minutes. The air wasn't at all stuffy or stale as I thought it might be, yet I felt a kind of relief when we climbed up to the surface and found ourselves standing by the woodpile.

Nancy, however, was terribly excited by the entire arrangement. She had a hundred questions to ask Eckman and the two of them stayed behind when Zeff, Savanna, and I climbed back out. It was a good twenty minutes later when they joined us in the kitchen where by now we were drinking beer and disassembling the chicken.

"I'd buy this place in a Dixie minute flat if I had the money," Zeff was saying, "but the price of farmland is going right through the roof. Every year it goes up something like twenty percent. But it sure beats the hell out of living in the city. A guy could put in some vegetables, like Eckman says, and maybe get a cow and a pig or two and you could just sit back and let the economy of the country collapse and it wouldn't make any difference."

"Somebody told me you didn't drink," I said to Eckman, watching him chugalug a beer.

"Usually I don't," he said cheerfully, "but this is a social occasion!" He wanted to know about me and about C.O.B.R.A.

"It isn't working out the way I planned," I told him. "Frankly, these street people are not much good to anyone, including themselves. They respond to an emotional appeal but none of them really have anything you can build on. Their actions are determined strictly by how they feel and none of them seem willing to admit that their thinking might be fucked up."

"Some of them are OK," Eckman said. "A lot of them are more honest than the bastards in City Hall."

I was surprised to see Zeff drinking some of the vodka I'd brought. I looked at him but didn't say anything. He noticed my glance. "I'll just have a sip," he said; "any more and I get sicker than a dog."

Suddenly Eckman blurted out: "Why don't you guys bring me out a half dozen or so of the rottenest people in town. C.O.B.R.A. shouldn't have any trouble rounding them up. Kick the shit out of them and haul 'em out here and we'll lock them all together in the trailer and see how they get along. Christ! wouldn't that be something to see! We could even get a movie camera and make ourselves a regular documentary. It'd be sensational. I'll bet you they'd turn on each other like mad dogs, just like during a riot in the joint when no guards are around!"

No one laughed, or even spoke for a moment. Finally: "Who do you have in mind?"

Eckman didn't need time to think. "Get that fat porno czar," he said; "we'll see how he likes it down there in the dark. Watch yourself, though, he carries a piece and he's always got at least one bodyguard with him.

"And grab one of those syphiloid whores off Hennepin. No, I've got a better idea: don't get the whore; follow her and nab a couple of her WASP johns. It'll be great to have some pillars of the community around! Nail the clown in the act so we can tell him he's full of syphilis bugs after he's here; that'll give him something to think about."

Nancy's eyes were shining. She took a long swallow of her boilermaker and watched Eckman, waiting to hear what he'd say next.

"And I wish to God I could get my hot little hands on some of these bible-pounders," Eckman went on. "There's an endless procession of them on Sunday morning TV--one right after another. Every one of them has those lunatic eyes--but, man, do they know how to hustle the bucks. Yes, sir, these guys have got to be the greediest, power-hungriest dogs in the whole goddamed sewer system. But, what the hell, I guess this is out . . . because all the really satanic ones come out of L.A., or the south. Well, let's see . . . " He opened another beer.

"Any oil company executive would be a legitimate bastard to punish, any prison guard, anyone connected with the liquor business . . ." Now Eckman thought of something else. "Did you know that there are hush-hush places all over the country maintained strictly to hold Roman Catholic priests who have committed sex offenses? Wouldn't it be neat to find out where one of them is and grab a couple of the pussy-lovers for our little zoo!" He started to laugh but a paroxysm of coughing overcame him. He dropped his can of beer and held his side while a thin film of sweat broke out on his reddened face. "They could ... could give sp ... spiritual guidance to the ... the others," he gasped weakly.

Later, when we were walking around the yard, I asked Zeff why he had mined the place. He said that he placed the first few charges to get the weasels that were after his chickens. "But then Eckman got me to put charges all over," he said.

"Do you do anything Eckman asks you to," I asked.

He shrugged. "He's got the money, Chris. When you've got money you give orders and when you don't have money you take orders. That's one of the facts of life."

I asked if any of the charges were powerful enough to kill a person.

"Not really," he replied. "Oh, I suppose the concussion could kill you if you were standing right on top of one, but, hell, they're really not much."

"Can you detonate them from the house, Zeff?"

"Most of them I can," he told me. "The ones by the chicken coop work by trip wires, though I have to admit I haven't got a weasel yet. I saw their tracks in the snow and they killed three of my chickens but so far they've been either smart or lucky."

Before we left, Nancy wanted to climb down into the trailer again and this time, alone, she stayed gone for nearly half an hour.

"What the hell were you doing down there, playing with yourself?" I demanded when she finally came up.

"I was just sitting down there thinking," she said; "just thinking and planning."

I didn't ask for details. It was time to head back to the city. "We'll see you guys later," I said to Eckman and Zeff. "And, Eckman, don't get discouraged; maybe we can do you some good!"

Savanna was a little too loaded to drive. So I got behind the wheel and we took off. "Crazy bunch of guys, eh!" Savanna said.

"I like them," I said. And I did.

"Do you like me too, Chris," he asked thickly.

"Get your hand off my knee, asshole," I said sharply. "Yes, I like you but you shouldn't drink so much."

"Neither should you!"

Of course he was right, so I said nothing.

* * *

Nancy's problem was solved with unexpected ease. Ever since returning from the farm she had been trying to come up with a scheme for getting Holmes out there without violence and with as few people knowing about it as possible. To physically overpower the man was possible; it would be easy enough to hire someone to sap him, but there was a risk involved here that Nancy was not willing to take. He was a very powerful animal and something could always go wrong. There was always the possibility that whoever she got to do it might talk or, worse yet, hit Holmes too hard and maybe even kill him. This would be the worst thing that could happen. Holmes must live; that was essential.

Obviously she was going to have to trick him some way or other. And soon. He appeared regularly at C.O.B.R.A. meetings but seldom spoke to others, choosing instead to sit by himself and merely listen. Savanna told her that he remembered Holmes' face from prison but had never associated with him.

The answer came on the night that Eckman showed up to speak. Chris had told him to come into town and give us some of his thoughts; like the ones he had expressed on the tape he made with Zeff. Eckman said he'd be delighted to and he came early, that night, cold sober and with a sheet of notes. There must have been about three hundred and fifty people present, drinking and blowing pot.

C.O.B.R.A. Meetings had become festive occasions. Now they were being held in a large American Legion hall on Nicollet Ave. and, along with a cash bar, there was a four-piece western band. At eight o'clock the band took a break and Eckman got up on the stage, unscrewed the mike so he could hand-hold it and walk about a bit, and started talking about his days in prison.

* * *

*Good evening, ladies and gentlemen. My name is Donald J. Eckman and I'm very happy to have the opportunity to speak to you tonight. I'm not going to stand up here and rant and rave at you because everything I've got to say can be said in a very short time and without any of the histrionics.

For starters, I want you to know that I've got cancer of the lungs and the doctors say I can expect to cash out at the end of summer or early fall. So I won't be around to see much of what's coming. And, frankly, my dear, I don't give a damn. Unquote. My opinions, right or wrong, are very strong. I'm not here to convert anyone, but I will say that I believe 100% in everything I'm going to tell you. Whatever else I am I'm no liar and I'm no phony.

The biggest phonies I ever met were the prison guards at the different joints I did time in. These are the lowest class assholes in the entire labor force. If they had any job skills at all they wouldn't be working for such pathetically low wages at such a risky and depressing job. But the jerks can't do any better for themselves. So they put on that ridiculous bus-driver's uniform and walk through the gates into the joint and for eight hours they're big shots. They can give orders, kick ass, and get away with saying things like: "Watch your mouth, nigger, or I'll throw you in the hole."

Tell me, where else can a high-school dropout get a job that gives him that kind of authority, that kind of power!

The same thing can be said for most women in this world who choose to have a whole bunch of kids. What other chance has your average female got to get herself into such a position of absolute power. Never mind all the crap about "I love children," or "I'm doing it for the greater honor and glory of God;" this is pure bull! Let's face it, there's a lot of satisfaction in bossing around other people, even little ones. There's a real sense of power in knowing they'll eat just exactly what you want them to eat, they'll go to bed when you say, they'll walk and talk and dress and work when, where, and how you want them to and, by God, they better toe the mark if they know what's good for them! Yes, motherhood has its rewards. And don't forget, it gives your average female something to do for twenty years. How else would she fill up the years of her otherwise stupid and pointless life!

And how else would prison guards fill up the eight hours they spend at the prison. Sitting in a bar? Shining shoes? Picking up empty pop bottles in the alley? Tell me! No, let's face it, these people just ain't got what it takes to compete. They can't go out there in the marketplace and get themselves a real job, a productive job, so they sit back there on the ass end of society like a leech and they suck for a living. The bastards are too lazy to work and too yellow to steal so they let the taxpayers support them. A prison guard! Dear God, what a shameful way of crawling through life!

They treat inmates like absolute shit. Oh, I don't mean every guard treats every inmate like a dog. But to the guard there is always a wall between the prisoner and himself--as though there were a vast and permanent difference. The guard doesn't know that the con is very conscious, perfectly aware of the fact the guard feels this way. And he finds it amusing. Often he is almost fascinated. Black people know exactly what I'm talking about . . . but let me get on with my story. Lots of cops are this way too. To them, everyone is either a good guy or a bad guy, one of us or one of them. They define everything in terms of absolute black or white because it's easier that way; it saves them the trouble of thinking, which they're too lazy or too stupid to do, and it eliminates the need to evaluate-- which could be painful.

Convicts have to live with this quirk of human nature. And finally, when they eventually get out, most of them just forget it and go on with their lives.

But mark my words, ladies and gentlemen, someday, somewhere, somehow, a convict with a memory is going to surface and strike back. One of the abused ones is going to retaliate. Oh, yes! And I don't mean some jerk is going to get a gun and shoot someone-- that's kid stuff; it happens every day. No, what I mean is that someone who knows how to think is going to find a way up there into the driver's seat and bring the whole system crashing down.

There are people in this world with a defective conception of time. Thirty years to them is like two weeks to you and me. This is a fact. It's scary but it's true. There is a wire hooked up in their heads, or there is a wire that isn't, and this is the kind of person that you are going to see rise like a rocket one of these days and raise more bloody hell than any sane person can even imagine.

Society is nowhere near as safe as most people like to think. Do you know how many policemen there are in this town? Less than six hundred. If these six hundred cops were all alone, tell me, what could they do against, say twelve hundred, or eighteen hundred, or five thousand of us! Can you imagine robbing a bank, for example, with five thousand armed buddies standing outside in the street! So the alarm goes off; so what! you've got all the time in the world. Who gives a rat's ass about six hundred cops. What could they possible do against five thousand armed men!

It's something to think about, eh! I'm not advocating anarchy. I'm not saying that some tightly-knit organization should get together and start making things happen. After all, I don't want to get arrested for inciting a riot. But I definitely am saying that organization is the key to maintaining, or changing, any social structure.

The Italians are the world's greatest organizers. They own, run, and control three of the most powerful outfits on earth: the mafia, the Roman Catholic church, and the Bank of America. You might not like Italians but you damn sure better respect them because anybody that ever tried to beat them at organization ended up broke, dead, or in prison--and don't ever forget it!

The world's worst organizers are women, American Indians, and Negros. They just don't know how to do it. They never learned, or they don't care, that two people working together are as effective as three people working individually. I'm not saying these people are stupid, I'm just saying they're ignorant, meaning they lack proper knowledge. They should study the Italians.

By the same token, the greatest masters of female psychology in America are the black pimps of San Francisco. These guys understand how a woman's mind works. True, they exploit this knowledge for their own gain, but the fact remains that they do know what women crave most. Not one loving husband in ten thousand is their equal in this respect.

My point is this: if you want to learn something, listen to an expert. And I am an expert who is telling you that the prison system in America, because of the way it's structured and staffed, is going to be directly responsible for producing an individual, and I mean very soon, who is going to bring the walls of Jericho tumbling down. Believe it; it's true!

Never have times been so ripe for this Creature from the Black Lagoon to step forward. The whole nation is becoming one gigantic cesspool. I see stuff on TV these days that would have been called obscene, unfit for public broadcast, just two years ago. I see secret groups, like this one, springing up all over. I see the international traffic in beautiful women growing by leaps and bounds.

Oh yes, this one of the things you never read about in the paper but it's getting to be a bigger and bigger thing right along.

Truly beautiful women are being abducted every day in major cities from coast to coast. From schools, from parking lots, from ladies rooms-- modern drugs, plus organization, make it ridiculously easy. And where are they sent? To the Middle East, to South America, to Africa. What is fifty or a hundred thousand dollars for such a valuable item in this day and age. And what are a few thousand miles, or ten thousand, with Lear jets so readily available!

Is this some fairy tale I'm laying on you? Like *hell* it is! It happens every day, including right here in Minneapolis. Just exactly where did you think these stunning women were disappearing to? Did you think they were all falling down wells?

* * *

Eckman, without saying another word, replaced the mike on its stand and walked off the stage. The room was quiet for a moment and then exploded in thunderous applause.

It was the pain in his chest that had forced Eckman to suddenly cut short his speech. There was a cot in the small dressing room behind the stage and he thought he'd lie down until it subsided. Almost at once, however, Nancy intercepted him. "Go find Savanna right away," she said, an urgent note in her voice. "Tell him to get Holmes back here right away. Go on, hurry. They know each other. Have Savanna tell Holmes that we want to hire him for a certain job."

"Do we?" Eckman asked, puzzled.

"It's a real slick way of getting him up to the farm," Nancy said. "We'll tell him that we're involved in procuring women like you were just talking about. We'll say that we're part of the pipeline; that we need someone to guard these two beautiful dancers till our contact gets here from Tampa. I've got a feeling that Holmes will go for this real big. Hurry up now. I'll put on my wig and take care of the rest."

Ten minutes later it was all arranged. "We need someone we can depend on," Nancy told Holmes. "Vince here says you were no snitch in the joint and you're big enough to handle any trouble. We'll give you a hundred and a half when the Florida dude gets here to fly them out and no one cares if you knock off a quick piece or two as long as you don't hurt them."

Holmes fell for it hook, line, and sinker. Savanna and Nancy agreed to pick him up the next morning at nine sharp at Duff's, on Ninth Street.

* * *

I myself didn't know they had nailed Holmes until after it was all done with.

Whether this was by design or accident I would never know for sure because it happened that I left the hall as soon as Eckman stopped speaking and when I finally returned to the apartment the next morning the three of them had already left for the farm.

What I did that night was drive out to the Black Dog power station, near the Minnesota River and, using armor-piercing ammo, I threw two clips of slugs into the bases of a few transformers. These were oil-cooled units and I knew that with the oil drained, they would short out and throw most of the city into darkness.

Of course, Northern States Power had a back-up supply of power which would cut in automatically within just a very few minutes but I didn't have any idea where this emergency power came from and I figured the morning paper would spell it out for me in great detail.

And this is precisely what happened. Over a leisurely breakfast at an Embers Restaurant the next morning I studied the map in the paper which diagramed exactly where the emergency supply of power was obtained. Elk River, Fargo, and the Trans-Canada line. I clipped this information and mused at the ease with which I had gotten it. Knowledge is power, I remember thinking, and now I had it!

* * *

Roosevelt Holmes was standing on the corner waiting when Nancy and Savanna drove up the next morning in the Ford van. It was a few minutes before nine.

"Right on schedule," Holmes remarked as he climbed in. He wanted to know how far it was to the farm.

"About an hour and a half drive," Savanna told him; "Why, are you too horny to wait?" Both men laughed.

This time Savanna drove west on Highway 7, a winding, picturesque road which roughly paralleled the route they usually took. Along the stretch by the lake great strands of fir and pine lined the road and, with many curves and hills, gave the impression that one was in Colorado, in the foothills of the Rockies, rather than in the midwest. Once past St. Bonefacious, the landscape flattened a bit and there was more open farm land. Savanna drove at precisely 55 mph, as he usually did, and Holmes was very interested in learning more about the women C.O.B.R.A. was procuring.

"Restrooms in downtown department stores are real good hit spots," Nancy told him, marveling at how facily she could lie. "I've got a mini-syringe I jab 'em with and if I inject the right amount of stuff I can make them so groggy they can barely walk in ten seconds or less. Then it's easy enough to help them to a waiting car and, bingo! we're on our way."

Holmes was fascinated. "What's in the syringe?"

"I don't have the vaguest idea," Nancy said. "I get it from some people in L.A. in small plastic bags. It looks just like water."

Holmes obviously had no trouble accepting this. "And you say most of the broads are sent to the Middle East, eh. To rich Arabs, I guess."

"I suppose so," Savanna said; "these guys have so much money they can buy anything they want and a lot of them are wild for big-boned, blonde American and Scandinavian women. But you have to remember, Holmes, that we don't know for sure where any one of them goes. We're just one part of the railroad. Once we turn them over to the next guy and get our money then we're out of it."

Nancy felt it was time to change the subject. She and Savanna had discussed this story only briefly and dwelling on it too long might require some details they were not prepared to present. Thinking ahead to when they would actually arrive at the farm, she did however feel it necessary to toss out one more item for safety's sake. "The dancers should be there by now," she said, speaking thoughtfully, as though mentally checking a timetable. "But then again they might not get in until tonight. I'm not sure but I heard they nailed them in Winnipeg, up north. Sometimes they're late getting in when they have to drive so far."

"You got members way up there?" Holmes asked.

This was the sort of question which could lead to complications, especially if Savanna should leap in with some imaginative reply. "They're not C.O.B.R.A. people," Nancy said quickly; "they're just some dudes who work with us now and then in exchange for a fast buck. Anyway," she went on, "the first thing I'll do, whether they're there or not, is show you where we keep them. It'll tickle the hell out of you. It's a buried trailer, see; a house trailer. It's buried underground and has electric lights, ventilation, the whole bit. Well . . . there's no running water but we keep two or three five-gallon cans of it down there. It's got beds, blankets, pots and pans, a hot-plate, . . . even a toilet. All the comforts of home you might say!"

Holmes chuckled. "Except they can't get out!"

"No way in hell," Savanna said. "If they managed to kick out a wall they'd find steel fence posts set in concrete six inches apart and there's boiler plate covering the roof and a quarter-inch steel door in front. Oh, it's a maximum security little joint all right!"

"Couldn't you just keep them in the house?"

Nancy was ready for this. "Too risky," she told Holmes. "There's always the possibility of noise--screaming and carrying on--and then you have to think of barking dogs and nosy neighbors and the sheriff . . ." She was warming to the subject. "But the main thing is that there's too many people coming and going at the farmhouse and some of them can't necessarily be trusted. This is one of those things that you're better off letting as few people know about it as you can. Some people talk too much. So we just play it safe. We can keep somebody in that trailer for weeks on end if we had to and nobody would ever find them or know anything about it."

By this time they were within ten miles of the farm. Savanna turned right, traveling north now, and in the accompanying slight lurch, Holmes let his left hand fall on Nancy's leg. Instantly her face heated but she forced herself to stare straight ahead. This was no time to flare up and blow the show. They were very close now. Nancy felt her heartbeat increase slightly and the faintest trace of a smile appeared. Yes, they were very close now, only minutes away.

Even before they turned into the driveway Nancy's eyes were darting around the yard. She was hoping it would be deserted, as indeed it was. Neither Eckman nor Zeff was expecting them and Nancy knew that had either man been in the yard they would have both approached at once. Even such friendly curiosity, however, could lead to complications.

"Go on in the house and see who's here," she said to Savanna as he shut off the ignition. "I'll take Holmes here and show him the trailer. We'll be right back."

She forced herself to laugh gaily. "Come on, guy, and get ready for a jolt. This going to knock you for a loop!" A moment later she bent and, seizing a bolted-down log end, lifted the hidden trap-door and swiveled it open. Holmes watched in genuine astonishment as she climbed down the ladder into the now exposed hole. "Follow me," she cried out, only her head above ground, "this is really great!"

Once at the bottom, Nancy quickly felt her way past the open steel door and into the trailer. She turned on two lights and then stood by the built-in kitchen table. Holmes was just reaching the bottom of the ladder and now he crouched slightly and came into the trailer. "Holy Jumping Christ!" he said softly; "you weren't bullshitting me, were you!"

"Hell, no, this for *real*! Well, the dancers aren't here yet but that's OK; it looks like everything is all ready for them. They'll probably get here tonight. Come on in; take a look at the back; that's where the master bedroom is."

Holmes, obviously impressed, walked past her slowly, looking around carefully and with great interest. When he was just entering the back bedroom, Nancy said casually: "I'll bring in these plastic water cans; I wonder if they remembered to fill them." Then, moving easily, she walked out of the trailer, swung the steel door shut, and snapped the heavy padlock in place.

As easy as that! she marveled, leaning against the cool steel door and looking up at the patch of sunlight above. My God! it only took five seconds! It's over and done; I've *got* him!

Eckman had cut a three-inch hole at eye level in the steel door. Turning, Nancy looked through it into the lighted trailer. Holmes was just coming out of the back bedroom. He showed no alarm. "Yeah, this is one cool setup," he was saying. "Hey! where are you, woman?" He reached the steel door and pushed on it lightly.

Nancy moved away from the door and over close to the ladder. "I'm right here, shit-ass, and you're right there; how does that grab you!"

Holmes rapped on the door with his knuckles. "Come on, man, open this mother-fucking door before I kick the shit out of it." He put his eye to the hole and looked out.

"Don't you understand, Holmes? This whole thing was a scam. You've been *had*, fool. We've got you where the hair is short, sucker; you've just been nailed to the cross, hear!"

Holmes continued looking out the hole.

"What you talking that shit for, baby. Shit! I don't know you. You must be crazy. Get Savanna here; I don't want no more jive-assing." Now there was a definite note of fear in his voice; he was no longer sure this was just a strange joke.

"I'm the one you deal with, not Savanna. You never raped Savanna, you goddamned worthless turd. Do you remember a white brick apartment house on East Lake of the Isles Boulevard on a July night after the Aquatennial parade? Second floor, no dead-bolt, a cat that bit you when you stepped on her tail?"

"YOU!" Holmes shouted, "you fucking right I remember now! You're the kicker and screamer. I should have clubbed your brains out, whore. But I will anyway when I get out of here."

"You should have done lots of things, asshole, but it's too late now. Club my brains out? No, your clubbing days are done with. And your raping days are done with too. You'll never fuck again, not on this earth you won't. You're a rat in a trap, black one, and there's no parole board to con this time. I'm your parole board now. I'm your warden and your parole board and your guard and your judge and jury too. I'm your GOD, Holmes, you understand that, your *God!*"

"You better lighten up, bitch; I'll tear your ass apart." Holmes' voice was trembling.

"Go fuck yourself, animal." Nancy turned and started up the ladder. Dead silence followed her as she climbed to the top and only as she was moving the cover back in place did she hear it. Out of the hole beneath her came an incredible scream of such horrible intensity, terror, and furious rage that it was as though Satan himself was entrapped in the bowels of the earth.

Nancy shivered, pushed the cover into place, and walked toward the house.

* * *

On a Tuesday evening, about twenty minutes before sundown, a farmer drove into Cecil Cohen's yard on an old Massey-Harris tractor and knocked on the door. He told Eckman his name was Floyd Schmiesing and said he was worried about something that sounded like explosions. "Ceece asked me to keep an eye on the place," he said, "and I was just wondering if there was some kind of trouble."

Eckman did not like the looks of the old farmer. "I've been setting out some contact mines and testing a few of them," he said. Too damn many burglars sneaking around. I aim to blow the piss out of any burglar comes prowling around this place."

"The HELL!"

"That's right. Remember that case

down there in Iowa where the owners rigged up a rifle so it'd shoot anybody who opened the back door of their house? A punk thief broke in, got shot in the leg, and then sued the farmer for setting an entrapment device and ended up with something like a sixty-thousand dollar award from the court."

"Ja, I remember something about that case," the visitor said, "but what's that got to do with the noises I been hearing?"

"I'm trying to tell you. I don't want Cecil losing his farm like those fools in Iowa did," Eckman said; "I'm going to scare those thieves away before they even get near the place."

"Mines," the farmer muttered; "my Lord, I don't know. Seems to me you might kill someone or hurt them real bad, same as that thing in Iowa."

"They're just big firecrackers," Eckman said; "all bark and no bite. No way in hell would I actually snuff anybody."

Scratching his chin thoughtfully, the farmer turned to go. "Who are *you*, he asked suddenly, looking back at Eckman who stood in the doorway holding the screen door open. "I mean, I've seen you around town a bit . . ."

"I'm Ceece's nephew. I'm just holding down the fort. Thanks for stopping by though."

"Ja, ja, just wanted to make sure that everything was OK. Well, good evening, sir. He touched the bill of his cap. Then he climbed back on his tractor and drove off.

"Nosy old fart," Eckman growled. He wondered if the farmer had Cecil's phone number in California; if he'd maybe call out there and get Cecil all worked up. Or now the sheriff might be coming around for a look-see. Oh, who gives a damn. I'll say I was just pulling the old man's leg; just having a little fun with the old bugger. Eckman grinned and let the screen door bang shut. Actually, officer, we've got rats in our woodpile and sometimes I take a blast at 'em with my 12-gauge!

* * *

It was noon. Nancy had been staying out at the farm since she snared Holmes and I had been laying low at the apartment, resting and thinking. I was unwrapping a smoked whitefish for lunch when the phone rang. "Chris," he said, "why don't you come with me to the Guthrie Theater this afternoon. They're having a matinee and I've got a couple of tickets." The Guthrie was an extravagant legitimate theater on the edge of the Minneapolis loop.

"I'm eating," I told him, "and, besides, I don't like plays."

"You've never seen one," he laughed, "not like this one, anyway. It's 'The Silver Tassie' by Sean O'Casey. What are you eating?"

"Smoked whitefish and strawberries."

"Let me pop over for a minute," he said, "I'll bring two cans of beer; that smoked fish is real salty."

"All right," I told him, "but don't plan on staying; I'm on a schedule."

He hung up and I stood there for a moment puzzled at what I'd just said and done. I had never liked to socialize with anyone and I certainly never invited people over. I had always been a loner, by choice, and yet here I had just broken my own, my firmest rule.

Well, I did like Savanna. He was a likeable cuss, and quick with his wits, and I guess a piece of fish and a beer was no big deal.

By the time he arrived, twenty minutes later, I had pulled all the meaty chunks of fish away from the bones—a task I thoroughly enjoyed—and piled them on a plate. The strawberries I merely rinsed under the cold water and dumped in a bowl, stems and all.

I was amazed, perhaps even a bit suspicious, at Savanna's high spirits. "Have you been drinking?" I asked him.

"No, hell no. I'm just feeling good about this play being here today. I don't usually read the morning paper but I did today and I just happened to spot the ad. I wish you'd come along, Chris; it's a real gripping play. I saw it over in Dublin a couple years back with

Philip O'Flynn, John Kavanagh, Maire O'Neill, and Kathleen Barrington."

I looked at Savanna curiously. "You've been to Dublin? I didn't know that." And I didn't; his record didn't show it."

"Lots of times, Chris. I haven't spent my whole life in jail!"

"How come you rattle off those Irish actors so easily," I asked.

"Because I'm a big fan of all of them. There was a time when I planned on going into theatre myself. Well, things didn't happen that way but I'll always love theatre. A good play is so superior to a movie that there simply is no comparison."

Impulsively, without knowing why, I said I'd go with him. "Here," I said, "chew on some of this smoked fish; it's good for what ails you. What's this Silver Tassie about?"

Savanna snapped open two cans of Grain Belt from the six-pack he'd brought and gave one to me. "It's an anti-war play," he said. "You see, a tassie is a loving cup, a trophy, and this football team, all young, tough, healthy guys, used to all drink from it when they won a game. When war came along--this would be World War 1-- they had a big celebration just before they went marching off to the trenches. They all looked at it as a splendid adventure, a very romantic chapter in their lives. Their girlfriends did too. But then they go into actual war and everything changes. God! Chris, wait till Act 2, when that gigantic cannon rises out of the floor and fires--it fires a deafening charge and belches out smoke and flame--it'll blow your mind!

"Well, the two main characters both get wounded. One loses his legs and the other is blinded. So the crippled guy has his wheel chair pushed around by his blind buddy and calls out directions to him. All the survivors of the war attend one final get-together at their old college and they smash the tassie up in rage and hatred for what they were never taught. Oh, it's some play, Chris; you'll love it!"

And as it turned out he was right. Not many times in my life have I ever been so moved by a single experience. Several times I found myself on the verge of tears during the play and glancing around I saw that many in the audience were openly crying. I mentioned this to Savanna as we left the theater and he responded sombrely, "I was one of them; didn't you see me wiping my eyes!" I had, of course, but I hardly expected him to admit it so openly.

"Don't you ever cry, Chris?"

"I haven't cried since I was four years old," I told him; "I can't afford to."

"Well . . ." he said hesitantly, "should we go back to your place and finish that beer?"

Again, without really thinking of what I was saying or doing, I agreed. So we walked through Loring Park, returning the polite greetings of several homosexuals we encountered, and arrived at Nancy's and my apartment just as the sun went down.

As we sat there drinking beer on the couch in the living room I asked Savanna why he had gone to Ireland.

"All four of my grandparents are from there," he said, "but I never went there because of that. It just happened that I found myself in New York City with a lot of money one time and while I was walking down Fifth Avenue I spotted an Aer Lingus ticket office and so I just strolled in and bought a one-way ticket to Shannon. I had my passport with me so there was no hassle and the next morning I was there. I was so dumb back then that I thought Shannon was a big city, not just an airport, but eventually I got to Dublin and I *loved* it. I've been back many times but there's only one first time and it was never to be quite the same again."

"Did you ever think of living there?"

"There's no way to make a living, Chris. The people are extremely poor. Christ! Ireland has the third lowest standard of living of all the forty-one countries in Europe; only Portugal and Greece are lower."

It was obvious to me now that I had pegged Vince Savanna incorrectly. There was more depth to him, and more charm, than I had ever suspected.

Now he opened another beer and gave me a wide grin. Want to fly over with me and check it out?"

"I've got things to do," I told him.

He was still smiling when he grabbed me by both arms. "We all have things to do," he said tenderly and the next instant he was crushing my lips with his mouth.

An electric shock ran through me. My back stiffened and I tried to cry out but already I was suffused in a glow of sudden pleasure and without even being conscious of it my arms reached around him instinctively and hungrily and I gasped in the lovely gush of wetness and warmth. Now, trembling and fumbling, he was undressing me and only for a fleeting instant was I aware that he would learn I wore silk panties. Then every semblance of rational thinking ceased as we both fell naked to the lushly shagged floor and let ourselves sink, with little fierce sobs of love, into a wildly delicious frenzy of perfect ecstasy.

Deep within me, half insane with passion, he slowed but once and face next to mine he cried: "Oh, Chris, my God, Chris . . . you're the most exciting woman I've ever known!"

And then, almost in unison, we both clenched our teeth and screamed.

* * *

Two days later Nancy had still not come back from the farm and Vince Savanna was still at my apartment. He never seemed to run out of questions concerning how I'd pulled it off for so many years.

"How in God's name did you ever get away with it in Korea," he had asked. "Out of all those men you'd think *someone* would tumble."

"That was the easiest part of all," I told him. "Remember, we were all dirty and stinking and shabby and in all the confusion and lack of order no one really paid that much attention to anyone else."

"How about when you had to go to the pot?"

"I sat on the little round hole just like everyone else. How do you think women shit, standing on their head?"

"But I'll damn sure bet you never took a shower!"

"You lose, Vince. I never did when it was real crowded but, yes, I did take quite a few showers. I'd wrap a towel around my butt going in and coming out and, sure, I'd jump into my o.d. skivvies fast but you'd be amazed at how people see what they expect to see. I never had any boobs to speak of and, what the heck, I was just another pink-cheeked 18-year-old; a modest one too!"

"What about your periods?"

"Ever hear of tampons. Come on,

Vince, believe me, there was nothing to it. Oh, I could have been nailed easily if I'd gotten sick or been wounded but I never actually cared if I got caught or not. And I'm not just *claiming* I didn't care, I'm telling you flat out that I honestly didn't give a tinker's damn. I figured it'd be my brother John's ass, not mine. I can get out of anything. Damn if I'd turn on the little-girl tears, no, not that; I'd stand up straight and tall like a good brave soldier and tell 'em I was only trying to do something noble for my great and wonderful country. Hell, I was only seventeen; what could they possibly do to me!"

Vince sat there thinking it over. "Now let me ask you a question," I said; "tell me how you knew."

He answered at once. "By your eyes and the smell of your skin."

"Go on with you!"

"I'm serious. I'm very sensitive to smell. The clean, washed body of a female emits a very distinctive odor and I couldn't possibly make an error in this area. Negros have a distinctive odor too . . . to me they do. It's not good and it's not bad, it's just distinctive. I can smell death too. I can walk into a room where someone has died even eight or ten hours earlier and I know it instantly. It smells something like ammonia and flowers. And I can smell fear six feet away. Honest! Fear has an odor as distinctive as bacon or onions. But never mind about that, I want to talk about if you'd gotten caught in Korea. You can bet they would have put your brother in Leavenworth. And maybe that's where he belongs. He sounds like a real prick.

"No, he isn't. He's a good kid. It's his mother whose guts I can't stand."

"Is she the one who made you so bitter?"

"Bitter? Me? I'm not bitter, Vince, I'm a realist. I know people and I've seen time and time again what they do and I meant every single word I ever said at those C.O.B.R.A. Meetings."

Vince could often reveal great compassion. "We're all victims of our experiences, Chris; you, me, Al Capone, Pope John . . ."

"Sure we are, and that's why I'm so glad I'll never have any kids. Don't you feel sorry for any kid being born into this crappy world today. Maybe some of them will have a fairly decent share of love and food but none of them can escape the evilness that surrounds and influences us. You can take a dog and make him into a pathological killer just easy as pie. Guys that own junkyards do it all the time. They take a young puppy and they jam red-hot cigarettes into his nose until the poor pain-crazed creature goes stark raving mad at the sight of a human being. Then they turn them loose in the junkyard at night and believe you me, buddy, that's what you call a first-class watchdog. I've walked past junkyards at night and I've seen those dogs with their scarred noses bite the chain-link fence till their jaws were bloody they were so insane to get at me. Remember that line from Jim Croce's old song: 'meaner than a junkyard dog'? Whoever wrote that line knows exactly what I'm talking about.

"And the same thing goes for these organ-grinder monkeys you see in the big cities. They wear those cute aprons with the big pockets and if you toss them a nickel or a dime or a quarter they'll bow and then pick it up and put it in their pocket for the grinder. But you know how it is if you toss them a penny. They get mad as a son-of-bitch. They shriek and chatter and jump up and down and then they pick up the penny and fling it back in your face with all their might. Do you know why they do this, Vince?"

"To make the people laugh; to make you throw them a bigger coin."

"No, no, no; monkeys don't give a shit if you laugh or cry. And all coins are the same to them except copper pennies. Because they associate pennies with pain. When they're real young the trainer heats pennies in a frying pan until they're almost red-hot. The little critter has already been taught to pick up coins and put them in his pocket. He knows he'll get a reward for doing it. So just when he's learned to associate coins with bananas the hot pennies are tossed to him and when poor Jocko picks one up he burns the hell out of his fingers. He learns to look twice at a coin before he grabs it and this is something he never forgets for as long as he lives."

"Don't you think there's a difference between dogs and monkeys and children?"

"In this area there isn't one speck of difference. Life burns us all and makes us what we are. To this day I crave the affection of older women—all because of my stepmother. Damn! what that woman did to me. You'd think that just as one female to another there would be some kind of bond but I promise you it doesn't work that way. Why she didn't just send me back to the county I don't know unless it was the seventy bucks a month they got for feeding me.

"Christ, that woman was really sick. One time I had my hair combed half over my face, ala Veronica Lake, and she grabbed a pair of scissors and just started hacking away. I screamed and howled and tried to sink my teeth into her but what can a grade-school girl do against a grown woman. She cut off five big fistfuls and, boy, was I a mess. Can you imagine how I felt when I had to go to school that way and face my girlfriends!"

"I couldn't even have toast for breakfast. Her Johnny could but I couldn't because electricity costs money and money doesn't grow on trees, unquote.

"Vince, I really mean it when I say I'm glad I'll never have any children. I'm too old now anyway but even if I wasn't I guarantee you I'd be the most horrible bitch of a mother you ever laid eyes on. You'd think a woman with a tough childhood would be the world's most loving mother but they're not. They are even meaner to their own kids than their mothers were to them--and the beat goes on!"

Vince was looking at me closely. "Chris, when you were overseas did you . . . did you ever . . . ah . . . well, have sex?"

"What difference does it make. Cripes, that's a long time ago, honey."

"But I want to know."

"Well, all right, yes, I did. But never in Korea. I was scared of VD and I was afraid someone might recognize me or find out. But when I went to Japan on R & R I put on girl's clothes a couple times and picked up an officer. There, now are you satisfied!"

"Not really," he said, laughing and taking me in his arms. "Come on, love, let's talk some more." He kissed me gently on the side of my neck.

"Where," I whispered.

"We'll find a place, dear one."

* * *

Six days after returning to the farm, on a sunny Saturday morning, Nancy decided that the time had some to take care of Roosevelt Holmes. She arose early, washed and dressed hurriedly, and was drinking her morning coffee at the kitchen table when Zeff came in from his morning visit to the hen house.

"I found twenty-one eggs," he announced cheerfully; "you want me to fry you up a couple?"

"I'm not hungry, Charlie," Nancy said; "I've got work to do."

"Boy, what a gorgeous day, Nancy. I counted sixteen ducks paddling around on the pond and those baby chipmunks are running all over the place. I tell you, you just can't beat life in the country. Especially the early mornings. Yes, sir, this is the day which the Lord hath made; rejoice and be glad in it, alleluia!"

Nancy looked at him sharply. "What's that?"

"It's a good day to be alive," Zeff said.

"It's a good day to castrate a nigger," Nancy replied.

Zeff had filled a pail of water at the cistern and had begun washing the eggs. Now he stopped and turned to study Nancy's face. "Are you really going to do it," he asked curiously.

"Will a bear shit in the woods? Yes, I'm really going to do it. And not only that, I'm going to *enjoy* doing it."

Zeff was silent for a moment. He turned back to washing the eggs. "You realize you might kill him, don't you. I mean, after all, you're not a surgeon."

"You don't have to be. I've watched my dad castrate pigs and it's only something like a ten-second job."

Zeff thought some more. "I know you've said before that you were going to but, well, it's something that I've just never been able to make up my mind about."

Nancy gave a little snort of distain. "You don't *have* to make up your mind," she said; "I made up my mind and that's all that matters." She got up and poured herself another cup of coffee. "And you don't have to worry about getting involved either, Charlie Zeff, because I'm perfectly capable of taking care of this all by my lonesome. And as soon as I finish this coffee that's exactly what I intend to do. When is the last time you gave him any water to drink?"

Zeff had to stop and think. "I didn't give him any at all yesterday, Nancy, so I guess it's at least two days now."

"No, I gave him one bottleful yesterday morning," Nancy said. "I hope Eckman didn't. Go wake Eckman up and find out for sure. Never mind, I'll do it myself." She got up and went into the living room where Eckman was sleeping on the sofa. A moment later she was back. "Eckman says he hasn't been down in the trailer in two or three days. That's just the way I wanted it. Our friend Holmes must be real thirsty about now." Nancy found two beer bottles and began filling them with water.

"He must be about starved to death too," said Zeff. Nancy had absolutely insisted that Holmes not be fed.

"No one starves to death in six days," Nancy said. "Even Christ went forty days and forty nights. Don't you read your bible?"

"I read it once; that's enough. Most of the characters are crazy and the plot is weak."

Nancy laughed and spilled some of the white power she was pouring into the bottles from a small white envelope.

"What in the hell is that stuff," Zeff asked.

"Chloral hydrate."

Zeff understood at once. "Better not put it in plain water; he'll smell it or taste it-- or both."

Nancy stopped. "Are you sure?"

"Sure I'm sure. Alcohol masks the taste, water doesn't. If you want to knock the guy out you better put it in full bottles of beer. Wait a minute, I'll get a couple for you." Going to the refrigerator he took out two bottles of Pabst and uncapped them. "And don't put in too much or you'll paralyze his heart."

"I know how much to put in, Charlie. I

had a girlfriend in Montebello who tended bar and she told me all about this stuff. Don't worry, I'm not going to kill the cocksucker, I'm just going to knock him out for a couple hours--just long enough to perform a little corrective surgery."

"What if he doesn't drink them," Zeff asked, looking at the bottles; "what if he doesn't want them."

"He'll drink them all right. When you're as thirsty as he is even hot piss would taste good." Nancy carefully wiped off the traces of white powder which had spilled around the rims and then put her thumb over the top and slowly tipped each bottle several times. "I don't want to shake these up or they'll start foaming over," she said, speaking as though to herself; "I just want to mix in the Micky Finn a little."

She got two more bottles of beer from the refrigerator and put them, unopened, into a paper bag. Then she put the two doctored bottles in the same bag and hunted for a bottle opener in the silverware drawer.

"Charlie, my boy," she said brightly, "Dr. Rausch is about to go into action! I'm going to drink one shot of vodka and take two Compoz tablets at the same time--that's what I always do when I'm on the spot and it works like a charm. The vodka stimulates me and the Compoz calms me and while my nerves are trying to unjangle themselves I do what I have to do with no sweat and no strain."

"I'll tell you one thing," Zeff said, "I sure as hell don't want anything to do with this thing. You do anything you want, lady, but include me out."

"Relax, kid. And have no fear, Dr. Rausch is here!" Nancy threw the two Compoz tablets in her mouth and swallowed the shot-glass of vodka in a single gulp. Then she picked up the sack with the four bottles of beer and started for the door. Hardly had the screen banged when she was back. "My God," she said, "I almost forgot!"

Going into the living room, she rummaged around in the carton of clothing and personal effects she had brought with her from Minneapolis and when she emerged she had a small wooden box in her hand. She grinned and waved it at Zeff. "My X-acto knife," she said. Again the screen door banged.

"Christ in heaven," Zeff murmured to himself, "she really, actually means it!"

A few minutes later Nancy was at the bottom of the shaft. Finding the five-cell flashlight she had left there, she flicked it on and let it shine through the hole in the steel door into the darkened trailer. There was always a chance Holmes might have heard her coming and would be waiting right behind the door. While she didn't think his hand would fit through the hole she knew his fingers could and she wanted to take no chances.

"Wake up, baby, the International Red Cross is here to check on your condition." In the beam of the flashlight she could see Holmes now. He was lying on a couch near the back.

He sat up and stared into the light. "Bring me some water, bitch. And bring me something to eat."

"I'm not a bitch, I'm your friendly Red Cross lady. The Geneva Convention sent me. Tell me, how have they been treating you in this place!"

"How about a cigarette."

"Sure, I'll give you a cigarette," Nancy told him. She threw three cigarettes and a book of matches through the hole. "I'll get you a couple ham sandwiches in about half an hour. I'll get them at the 7-11. Believe it or not we don't want you starving to death on us. Hungry, yes; starved to death, no."

Holmes snapped on the light, picked up the cigarettes and lit one, inhaling hungrily. "I want some goddam water," he said.

"You want, you want. Too bad about what you want, Holmes. You just had some water two or three days ago. What the fuck do you think this is anyway. You want a beer?"

"Fucking right I do; you got any?"

"Yes. Come on up to the door and I'll give you a beer. That'll make you thirstier than you were before. Nancy was uncapping a bottle just as Holmes put his eye to the hole.

Sticking the neck of a treated bottle through the hole, she held on to the newly opened one. "I'll have one with you," she said.

Nancy could clearly hear Holmes gulping the beer on the other side of the door. In a matter of seconds he had finished it. "Give me another one," he said.

"Maybe I will and maybe I won't," Nancy said. "But first, hand me back that empty bottle. I don't want you to go cutting your wrists on me."

"Crazy cunt. There's knives in the drawer here if I want to do that." He stuck the bottle through the hole. Nancy took it, uncapped another bottle and again handed him the beer with the chloral hydrate. She said: "Holmes, that story you told me a couple days ago about Hans Butterfield checked out. And so did the one about the gal in the parking lot, Marlene Joice. If there's anything else you've done you better tell me about it now."

"That's all there is to tell. I just got out of the joint. The police know all about the other stuff. Gimme another beer."

"You've had enough. I don't want you to start puking and messing up a good trailer. Tell me, how could you do such a thing to a young woman who never did you any harm. Didn't you ever stop to think of her family, her little children?"

Holmes said nothing. He walked back to the couch where he had been lying and sat

224

down heavily, the nearly empty bottle of beer in his hands.

Nancy talked through the hole. "And how about that little Butterfield boy. He was only six. For Christ's sake, think of what you did to him. He'd just made his First Communion. You not only committed mayhem on him, you took his life. You ended everything, animal; all the hopes and dreams and the might have beens. Don't you have any shame at all? Don't you have even one spark of conscience in your whole filthy soul?"

Holmes was drooping badly. His head dropped lower and lower and the beer bottle slipped from his fingers to the floor. Suddenly he snapped his head up sharply, looked toward the door, and tried to speak. Then he slid off the couch and crumpled in a heap.

For a full five minutes Nancy sipped on her beer, watched Holmes carefully through the hole in the steel door, and waited. Finally, convinced there was no chance at all he was merely acting, she unlocked the door and went in. She nudged his head with her toe and it rolled easily. Yes, Holmes was definitely unconscious.

Moving rapidly now, Nancy took the small wooden box from the paper sack, opened it, and set it on a nearby chair. Then she loosened Holmes' belt and, with considerable effort, pulled off his pants and his shorts. Holmes was stretched out flat on his back, his arms at his side. His eyes were closed and he breathed shallowly.

Now Nancy took out the small silver X-acto knife and, holding the front of Holmes's scrotum high in order to tighten the skin, she made a swift, neat, two-inch incision in the sac and then, calmly, popped each teste out the opening and with quick, easy movements cut it from the body. Each teste was about the size of a large walnut. Nancy set them carefully to one side and paused for a moment.

So far so good, she thought. Only seven seconds work and the job was already half done. There was scarcely any blood but Nancy knew that all this was about to change very fast. Again she reached into the small wooden box and this time she took out a needle with a length of thread attached. The thread was already knotted at the end.

Nancy's mouth was dry and she knew her heartbeat had speeded up but this was the moment she had craved and waited for and it was with a fierce joy that she seized Holmes' penis firmly and, with four strong slashes, cut it off at the base. Instantly a great flow of blood began. Pinching the skin in the area, Nancy picked up the needle and quickly made half a dozen stitches. The spurting veins were clearly visible and, making no attempt at neatness, she sewed stitch after stitch until the bleeding was slowed to an oozing trickle. Only then did she rise to her feet. Her hands and forearms were covered with blood. She wiped them on a small towel hanging over the sink and stood there looking down at Holmes.

"Never again, asshole; never again!"

There remained but one final detail. Reaching in the back pocket of her jeans, Nancy took out a hand printed sheet of paper she had prepared before and taped it to the mirror over the kitchen sink. The note read:

Rosie, Dear,
Five pain pills in cup. Take a few.
Better get your sweet little ass
to a hospital real fast. Door is
open. Lots of luck, sweetheart,
and don't come near this place
again or we'll blow your fucking
brains out.

She put the bloody penis and testicles in the paper sack and left, leaving the steel door wide open. Back in the house she said: "Come on, you guys, we better go into Minneapolis for a day or two."

Eckman said, "What the hell did you do to him?"

"I made him into a girl," Nancy said. "Here, take a look at this." She opened the paper sack and held it out.

"Jesus H. Christ!" Eckman said faintly. He looked like he was going to be sick.

"Let's *make* it," Nancy said again. "I'm

warning you, he's going to come around in less than an hour and he's going to be crazy wild."

"Shit, yes," Eckman said, grabbing his jacket, "I'm with you; let's go."

Zeff remained seated. "I'm staying right here," he said. "I'm not running from anybody. He's far too weak to hurt me anyway. Besides, he kind of likes me; I let him read a couple of my manuscripts."

"Do it your way then," Nancy said. "Me and Eckman are cutting out. We'll see you in a couple days." They ran out to the van and got in. "Have you got a gun, Charlie?" Nancy called out.

I've got a shotgun of Ceece's but there's no shells for it," Zeff shouted back.

"As long as he doesn't know that then you can bluff with it if you have to," Nancy said. "'Bye now. Remember, the steel door and the trapdoor are both open and he'll be coming out in about an hour." They drove off.

Zeff sat down in the kitchen and started writing in his journal. He wrote: Something very unusual happened today . . .

* * *

On the afternoon that Nancy came back to the apartment I was glued to the TV watching Bob Eubanks M.C. "The Newlywed Game." With disgust and fascination I watched him roll his eyes and ask the pitiful morons:

"How long did you know your wife before you made whoopee together?" The audience roared with appreciative laughter when one crude oaf responded, "Three hours!"

I waited for Eubanks to ask: "And how much did she charge?" but he only recoiled in mock horror and rolled his eyes again in thinly-disguised delight. God, how I despised this creature. He wore the perpetual leer of a nasty little boy who, having just discovered sex, spent all his waking hours playing with himself through a hole in his pocket.

The contestants were even sorrier. Carefully selected from the lowest of the low class, they gave every viewer the absolute right to feel superior to them as they shamelessly revealed their most intimate secrets in exchange for the opportunity to win a dishwasher or, more frequently, a color TV set on which, presumably, they could watch other ridiculous fools humiliate themselves for the titillation of the mob.

Nancy came in, looking disheveled and a bit flushed. "Hi, Chris," she said; "are you watching that stupid program again!"

"It's the masochist in me," I told her. "I can't believe this country has sunk so low that shit like this is permitted on the air."

Nancy went in the bathroom and began filling the tub. "Then why do you watch it?

"For the same reason I went to see 'Jaws' and 'The Exorcist'. Because I'm interested in keeping track of what America is interested in. Anytime twenty million or more people come up with the collective opinion that something is great then I have to see it or hear it in order to keep my finger on the pulse of the people. But that doesn't mean I have to like it, and I usually don't. This program, for example, is sick. And I thought 'Jaws' was something for five-year-olds. Christ! I've read comic books more exciting than that stupid thing. A big shark swims in from the ocean and starts biting people. So what! I mean, who gives a rat's ass. What am I supposed to do, fall apart at the seams and go running for mommy? "Oh, mommy, mommy, the big shark is trying to bite me in the ass, wah, wah, sob, sob. Shit! The most fantastic part of all is that there are enough illiterate slobs out there to turn a low-grade bubble-gum flick like this into a box office smash. Remember that, Nancy; remember when you deal with Americans today you're dealing largely with idiots. Sad but true. Show me a human being and I'll show you an asshole!"

"Let me show *you* something," Nancy said, coming out of the bathroom and picking up the paper sack she had brought back from the farm. "It's not an asshole but it's pretty close to it!" She laughed and, opening the sack, thrust it at me.

It took a moment or two for the smelly, bloody message to sink into my brain.

The room swayed slightly and I knew my voice was trembling.

"Holmes?" I asked.

"Yes. Holmes! I said I was going to do it and I did!"

My stomach was churning. "Nancy, I don't like to say this but I'm going to say it anyway: you're sick."

"Are you kidding, I never felt better in my life."

"But . . . this is *murder!*"

"Like hell it is. He's not dead and he's not about to die. I left the door open so he could get to a hospital right away. Don't worry, if I wanted him dead he'd be dead, but I want that son-of-a-bitch to live. That's the only way I know for certain that he's suffering. After all, maybe there is no hereafter . . . so I want him to have his hell right here on earth. I want him to see a world full of pussy that he can never have. I want him to stare at Penthouse centerfolds and scream with rage. I want his voice to turn soprano and I want him to get fat and lazy like a eunuch . . . because he is one. Oh, yes! that's what I want and that's the way it's going to be!"

"He'll think I arranged it," I said slowly. Now it'll be me that he's out to get."

"I don't follow you."

"You said he remembered you after you locked him up, didn't you. You said he called you the kicker and screamer after you reminded him of the white apartment on Lake of the Isles. That means the scene is fresh and straight in his mind now and no way is he going to forget me. He probably even knows it was me speaking at C.O.B.R.A."

"I refuse to believe that," Nancy said; "he's not that smart."

But I was certain I was right. "He maybe didn't recognize me at the time," I said, "but he's seen you and me together lots of times and now that he knows who you are he'll put two and two together. He might be ignorant but he's not stupid."

Nancy saw my point. "What are you going to do about it, Chris? Why not just call the police."

"I can't. He'll charge you or me or both of us with kidnapping and mayhem. Savanna too. If we leave him alone he might leave us alone because he knows we know about Marlene Joice and the Butterfield boy."

Nancy was bound and determined to be cheerful. "Tell me you're proud of me, Chris; come on, say it!"

"I wish you hadn't done it, Nancy. You're rocking the boat. You've complicated things. I told you before to forget about that punk. He's not worth the trouble he can cause us. If word gets around those black dudes in C.O.B.R.A. that we did this to him our ass is buttermilk. The whole damn bunch of them—black and white both-are nothing but freaks and dopers anyway. I'm through with them. They're too rowdy and there's no way to get them into any kind of order. You can't unite them for a common purpose because they're minus all the basic tools you need to work with. As a group they're scum in anybody's book. No wonder that conquering armies always kill all state prisoners as they advance into another nation; trouble-makers are no good to anyone and all the C.O.B.R.A. people are nothing but trouble-makers temporarily on this side of the bars."

"Well, I'm going to take a nice, hot bath," Nancy said. "As they say, there's blood on my hands." She went in the bathroom and shut the door.

But I had a few things more to say. Nancy had shut off the water now and I knew she could hear me clearly as I stood by the door. "What's done is done, Nancy, but personally I think it's sickening."

"Is it any more sickening than what you did to that guy out there in that minefield in Korea?"

Apparently, Nancy wouldn't see the difference. "That was different. It was impersonal. I didn't even know him. He had something I wanted and there weren't any feelings involved."

"Holmes had something I wanted too," Nancy shot back. And it was plenty personal. So what's the difference. Quit rationalizing."

"I never do anything involving persons or personalities," I explained. "I only deal in abstractions. Mobs of people are an abstraction, like a pile of maggots."

"Go away and leave me alone," Nancy said.

My face got hot. Moving quickly into the living room, I snatched up the paper bag, slammed open the bathroom door, and held it out to Nancy. "And just what am I supposed to do with this mess," I demanded.

Nancy leaped out of the tub. Naked and dripping wet, she seized the sack from me, dumped it in the toilet, and flushed it. The toilet almost clogged.

"There," she said, climbing back into the tub, "that takes care of that. Simple problem; simple solution!"

I turned to go. "Tell me something, Nancy; why did you do it? Really. Did you hate him that much?"

"Yes," she replied, "and I loved you that much; you're the only sister I've got."

I stood there for a long moment looking down at her. "My little Nance," I said softly, "I love you too. But I swear to God, kid, the way you carry on sometimes, a person would think it was *you* who got raped!"

Nancy flared a bit. "I was right there, Christian. I had to watch. It's the same thing!"

I left her then. "Not exactly, honey," I

said gently; "not exactly."

* * *

It was one of those gorgeous, absolutely perfect California mornings such as one rarely sees more than five or six times a year. It had started raining shortly after midnight and continued until nearly four. Then, in the last hour before dawn, the light rain became a downpour. It thundered down on the old house in Whittier, swept the paper cups and the taco wrappers from the streets, and washed every trace of smog from the air.

At six-thirty, when he awoke to the thump of the L.A. Times landing on the front porch, Cecil Cohen knew at once what it would be like. He could smell the fragrance of the orange tree just outside his bedroom window. Already the mocking bird who lived in it was decorating the day with its astonishing, never-sung-twice songs.

Dressing rapidly, he went out into the yard and took a deep breath. California in the morning! how wonderful it was. So clean, so peaceful and lovely, so sensual! How easy it was to stand here in the quiet dawn and imagine how it must have been a hundred years earlier. A veritable paradise. No wonder the Indians did nothing but lie under the trees sunning themselves and wait for the lucious plump fruit to fall. Why work! Why sweat and strain when everything was free in this pure, silky Shangri-La.

Then the white man came and ruined it all. Now the orange groves were gone, Mt. Baldy's snowy top was hidden in the yellow cloud for months on end, and the once magnificent coast was desecrated.

And yet, on mornings such as this, Cecil could clearly see how it once had been out here and it saddened him that it would never be that way again. In two hours the industrial machine would start up again, poisoning the air. The roar of a million Hondas hurtling down the freeways would drown out the songbirds, and by twelve noon The Third Horseman would be back in the saddle again.

But for now it was beautiful. Cecil glanced at his watch and saw that Rick's would be opening in ten minutes. Rick's was a restaurant on Greenleaf and Penn, just a five-minute walk from the house. Cecil liked to sit at a table by himself, have a leisurely cup of coffee, and enjoy a cigarette while he read Jack Smith's column in the Times. No two ways about it, Smith was the best columnist in North America. Nobody else was even close. As far as that goes, Cecil had decided, the L.A. Times itself was far and away the best paper he had ever read. It was almost worth moving to California just to be able to have it handy.

At seven o'clock sharp, when the head

cook unlocked the doors at Rick's, Cecil was there waiting with the handful of other early birds. With coffee only twenty-one cents and unlimited refills permitted, Rick's never lacked for customers.

Nearly an hour later, on his third cup and midway through the letters to the editor, Cecil looked up to see two men standing by his table. They were middle-aged and well dressed.

"Cecil Cohen?" one of them asked.

"Yes, that's me. What is it, gentlemen?"

One of the men opened a small leather foldcase and showed a card and badge. "We're from the Los Angeles County Sheriff's Office, Mr. Cohen. We'd like to speak with you a moment."

"Sure, sure. Sit right down." Cecil gathered up his paper. "What can I do for you?"

"You are the owner of the eighty-acre farm on County Road 107 just north of Winsted, Minnesota?"

"Yes, that's right. I am. I'm staying here at my sister's place just over on Comstock."

"Yes, we know; we were just there. Mr. Cohen, there's been some trouble at your farm."

"Trouble, eh. What kind of trouble? Fire? The house caught fire?"

"No, nothing like that. There's been a killing."

Cecil was speechless. One of the men glanced at the other and then continued. "A man identified as Charles Wayne Zeff was found murdered at your farm."

Cecil was badly shaken. "Someone shot Charlie Zeff?"

Again the two men exchanged glances. "He wasn't shot; his throat was cut with a kitchen knife."

"Oh my God . . . poor Charlie . . . he was one hell of a nice fellow . . ." Cecil's day was ruined.

"The authorities in Minnesota want to talk to you about the matter. Mr. Cohen. Would you like to return voluntarily?"

"Do I have any choice," Cecil asked. "Hell, I don't know anything about this—other than what you just told me. I was planning on staying here a couple more weeks. Are you placing me under arrest?"

"Not unless we have to," one of them said.

Cecil thought for several moments. "Maybe I'll just tell you to go to hell," he said finally; "that way the Carver County taxpayers can pay for my plane ticket!"

The next day, late in the afternoon, Cecil flew into Minneapolis-St. Paul International Airport and was met by two detectives from the county attorney's office.

Several times in the next few hours of questioning Cecil nearly told the men about the phone call from Floyd Schmiesing. But each time he changed his mind just as he was about to relate Floyd's story about all the mines that he said were planted. Floyd was probably mistaken. No sense bringing up something he couldn't be sure about. Still, maybe he ought to get it on the record just to be on the safe side. But it did seem rather far-fetched, even a bit silly. Better to not mention it.

"This fellow, Zeff," one of the detectives was saying, "he was a writer?"

"He was a lot of things," Cecil said, "but, yes, he was a writer. He had written quite a few books. He had a lot of manuscripts up at my place in fact."

"We know. We found them scattered all over."

"Let's start at the beginning," the other detective said. "Why did you move out of your house in the first place, Cecil?"

* * *

Vince Savanna was turning out to be a disappointment to me. Sexually he was no better and no worse than any other male, I suppose, yet he often failed to perform altogether. I told him to lay off the cigarettes; that I had read that nicotine had been proved to contribute to male impotence, but he only cursed at me and lit another Marlboro.

These times he failed me were a source of annoyance and considerable frustration but, still, they didn't bother me nearly so much as I'm sure they bothered him. Sometimes he would lie very quiet and feign sleep and other times he would get quite ugly.

After Nancy came back I didn't let him stay at the apartment anymore. Nancy probably wouldn't have cared but with our beds only a few apart I'd have felt uncomfortable. So Vince returned to his place in Kenwood and usually came over sometime around noon.

More and more I was realizing that this thing between him and me was merely a pause in a headlong flight, a space between acts, a plastic rose in a dusty bowl. Maybe if we both were younger or maybe if I knew more--or didn't know so much--or maybe if I hadn't already begun to tire of the world . . . maybe, maybe, maybe; who cares.

The biggest let-down was in learning that there wasn't much depth to the man. He was pragmatic and materialistic and so was I of course but I often spent time thinking about things other than money and today. I was fascinated by grand views and overlay images, by time, space, and grand scopes beyond the immediate moment. But Savanna had nothing to say about such matters.

"I'm living the last chapter of my life,

Vince," I told him once; "and it's by choice. I never thought I'd see the day when I could say with total honesty that I'm tired of the world and yet that's exactly how I feel today."

"You're just a little depressed," he said; "tomorrow you'll be OK."

"I'm not depressed at all," I told him. "I've been this way for a number of years and tomorrow I'll feel the same. One of the psychological differences between men and women is that women fear the future but they feel perfectly capable of handling today. To a man, though, the future always looks rosy; it's today that he's worried about. So when you put two people like this together they comfort one another and both lives roll along a little more smoothly. But, Vince, there is no man on the face of this earth who is going to comfort and console me about tomorrow. Because I know better. If things are a little tough today then you better believe it when I tell you that all the hardship and suffering in the world is nothing, absolutely *nothing*, compared to what's coming."

Maybe Savanna agreed with me or maybe he simply didn't know what to say but, at any rate, I gave him credit for remaining silent.

I continued. "The saddest part of all is that it could have been so beautiful. Can you picture a world full of cozy little houses with healthy, laughing children of all different colors playing together. Can you imagine everybody with enough to eat. Can you see them all fishing and tending their gardens and helping one another out!"

"Then it wouldn't be earth, Chris. Problems are part of the basic idea. Problems give people choices and making choices gives everybody an opportunity to develop themself, to become better."

"Yes, but there are enough natural problems without people turning on each other and manufacturing new ones."

Savanna looked at me and said: "How about you. Didn't you create a problem when you put C.O.B.R.A. together?"

"I'm going to disband them," I said promptly. This was something which had been causing me increasing concern.

"You can't," Savanna said matter-of-factly. "They won't listen to you any more. What do you plan to do, have them turn in their T-shirts? Ha! That gang is way far beyond any control you ever had over them. They're a real, genuine cult now. Thirty or forty bikers have come into the ranks and I tell you this whole group has turned into a vicious and dangerous bunch. There's something like twelve hundred people in it now. They've found something they can identify with and nobody--no cop or law or certainly not *you* are going to put a leash on them. Christ! they're a regular army! Last night when the bars closed they smashed every window on Hennepin Avenue from Thirteenth street to Washington Avenue. And you think they'll listen to you? No, Chris; you lit a fire you can't put out this time!"

I knew that most of what Savanna said was true. "OK," I said, "I'll buy that. I'll say that you're right and that I happen to agree with you one hundred percent. But they still know who I am and they'll still listen to me when I speak and so I'm going to exploit their wild asses one more time. I'll take the worst part of this whole situation and make it my greatest asset. If these assholes are as crazy and dangerous as you and the cops and the newspapers say, then everybody must be scared shitless of them. Let's cash in on that fear, Vince!"

He stood there and waited expectantly.

"Set up a meet between me and some people," I said. "First off, I want to talk to Skorpios, the porn king."

"That might be kind of tough, Chris. He doesn't exactly walk the streets and they say he's always got at least one armed bodyguard with him."

"Oh, you'll manage it somehow. If nothing else, grab his brother, Georg. He shows up at the Edgewater Inn almost every afternoon during happy hour."

"I'm supposed to do this myself? Grabbing people isn't my thing, Chris; you know that."

"Hire a couple apes from C.O.B.R.A. Just set it up and make it work. And scout around for a couple more people for me to talk to. I'm going to boil things down to a few individual personalities."

Savanna asked what I had in mind.

"I'm going to ask them to back off," I told him. "If I've got the ability to convince a handful of people then maybe I can convince larger numbers later on. And if I can't even get one or two people to buy my line then I might as well forget it.

"Vince," I said, "I'm not going to go into all the details but I promise you I can bring this city to its knees if I want to. And I do want to—but not without giving them the benefit of the weakest shadow of a doubt. The consequences to myself resulting from my own actions is entirely irrelevant, meaning I honestly do not care. For me all the illusions are over. I have only one more door to pass and I intend to march through it with my head held high and no regrets.

"So you fix it up for me with that Skorpios character," I went on. "And then in a day or two I want you to round up some other people for me. I want a WASP john, like Eckman suggested that time we were up there, and I want a gay bible-pounder, a big oil company executive, and maybe a pervert priest."

"My God, Chris, you're not . . . you're not going to do a *number* on them?"

"No, no, no—I told you, I'm just going to talk with them. I want to find out if people like me have any chance at all to live in a world we don't hate."

"You're not cracking up, are you, Chris? I mean, sometimes you give the impression that you wield some kind of divine power; like you are the judge and jury of the whole human race."

At that instant I stopped liking Vincent Savanna. Not a flicker crossed my face to reveal it but as far as he was concerned my heart had turned to stone. He was still useful to me but I'd never let him close to me again.

"No, I'm not cracking up," I said, making myself speak lightly. "And there's no such thing as divine power—not in my book. I'm just ten more toes walking down the same old yellow brick road that everyone else is on. Only I play for keeps, buddy; remember that!"

I opened the door for him to leave. "I'll get right on it with Skorpios," he said; "give me a couple days to work it out."

After he left I phoned E. F. Hutton Co. and asked how my silver futures were looking. When I learned December silver had jumped over seven dollars an ounce I damn near passed out. I'd been hoping for a fifty-cent rise, maybe eighty cents or a dollar at the most.

"Sell everything," I shouted into the phone. "Sell the whole works and no sand-bagging either; drop it in one move!" Then I hung up and stared at blank space. I had contracts for fifty thousand ounces! At seven bucks an ounce profit . . . my God! in a matter of a few hours I'd be worth a third of a million dollars! If only this were twenty years ago, or even ten . . . But it wasn't. It was the spring of 1979 and I was old. I was old and tired and money couldn't buy back the days that were gone or the dreams that had died.

I poured myself a small scotch and turned on the TV. The Newlywed Game was about to start. Tonight I would go out to the waterworks and check my antennas.

* * *

Getting to talk to Skorpios proved to be no problem at all. Savanna merely went into one of the man's pornographic bookstores and, while being carefully scrutinized by the clerk, copied down the address of the registered owner from the business license hanging on the wall, and then walked out. Municipal law required these licenses to be posted in a prominent place and I personally thought it was a good law.

I called his office, identified myself as the head of C.O.B.R.A., and asked for an appointment. I was told to come at five-thirty that afternoon. For reasons he did not explain,

Savanna did not want to accompany me and so it was Donald Eckman and I who showed up at Skorpios' office, which was located in a rather large brick building on East Hennepin.

Ushered in by a pair of silent, grim-looking men, we found ourselves in front of a bushy-haired, heavy-set man of about sixty who was sitting behind an old wooden desk. He was holding a copy of Variety and reading something in it very intently.

"Sit down," he said in a surprisingly soft voice; "what can I do for you?"

"I'm the head of a group of people here in town called the Cabal of Book of Revelation Angels," I told him. "We have about twelve hundred active members."

He looked at me and shrugged. "So?"

Now I picked my words with great care. "Not long ago a mob of these people went a little haywire and smashed every window on Hennepin Avenue. I'm sure you know all about that little incident."

"Sure I know about it. What's your point? Get to the point; I'm a busy man."

"The point is, Mr. Skorpios," Eckman said, "that a whole bunch of people don't like you or what you stand for and you may find very shortly that some rather dramatic changes are about to take place."

Skorpios threw aside the trade paper he had been holding and lit a cigar. Still speaking calmly he said: "I consider that a threat. And nobody threatens me, folks. Or, to put it a bit more accurately, nobody's threats bother me. Do you have any idea how many times I've heard this crap? Do you realize how boring I am finding this conversation! For you it's probably a brand new experience but, me, I've heard it all ten thousand times before.

"Listen," he said, speaking more forcefully now, "I'm going to tell you this just once and then you're going to get the hell out of my office. I'm a businessman. I obey the law, I pay my taxes, and whether you two know it or like it, I happen to supply a need to the people of this city. I give them something they want and are willing to pay for and I do it legally. If anybody doesn't like me or what I do then that's their problem."

"You're not making matters any better," I told him. "Basically, we want to ask you if you'll close all your bookstores and X-Rated theatres and help make this a better city."

Skorpios leaned toward me slightly and I was impressed by the fierceness of his eyes. "I don't consider that to be my primary obligation," he said. "I take care of myself and my family. The general welfare of humanity I leave to others. People like you two have a lot of guts walking in here and laying any kind of idealistic shit on me. I have tapes of both of you ranting and raving away in the park and it's perfectly obvious to me that it's *you* who are the problem, not me. Anybody can find fault, anybody can criticize, anybody can condemn and mock and tear down, and that's all you people do. Don't be coming around here jumping on me because I won't stand still for it. I can handle you people real fast and real easy. And if it's a better world you're worried about then I suggest you forget about the other guy and start with yourself because instead of being part of the solution, the way you seem to picture the thing, you're actually part of the problem. Now get the fuck out of here, both of you, or I'll break your goddam faces."

Eckman's voice was trembling when we got back to the street. "I'll take care of that fat bastard," he said; "I'll make him sorry he ever saw Ellis Island."

I remained silent. Deep in my heart I knew there was a lot of truth in what Skorpios had just said. If he had not set up his string of bookstores and movie houses, then someone else would have. Somehow, Skorpios seemed to me to be merely a shrewd opportunist. The truly evil people seemed to be those who supported him. And it was the city who supported him by their laws, their patronage, and their indifference. Yes, it was the city that was evil and therefore it was the city that must suffer. And what of those citizens of the city who may have done no wrong? The answer to that, of course, was the same given me by teachers from long ago who, when they were unable to determine which of us was the culprit, would punish the entire class and then tell us: "It is better for the innocent to suffer than the guilty escape!"

Now I was glad we had visited Skorpios; I felt better.

* * *

Roosevelt Holmes was hospitalized for eight days. When he stumbled into the emergency room at Metropolitan Medical Center, doctors examined him and attempted to question him but he would tell them nothing except his name, address, and phone number. While they were attempting to get more detailed information he fainted. A specialist from the Mayo Clinic was called in and, in a three-hour operation, Nancy Rausch's crude butchery had been surgically corrected. Holmes was placed in a private room but there was little more that could be done other than administer heavy doses of antibiotics and monitor him closely for infection while he healed.

During this time a police detective came to the hospital to speak to Holmes about several sex crimes which had occurred since Holmes had been released from prison. This detective, a young Negro man, spoke with

Holmes' doctor first and was visibly shaken when informed of the nature, and extent, of Holmes' injury. Since there was no evidence connecting Holmes with any recent crime, the questioning was cursory and the detective spent most of the ten minute visit inquiring, as the doctor had asked him to, about details of Holmes' emasculation. He learned nothing. Holmes would merely shut his eyes, turn his head to the wall, and not reply.

Almost from the beginning a stoic resolve had filled Holmes. Although he could not be sure who had actually disfigured him, he was convinced it was Chris who had made the arrangements, who had set him up, and who was responsible for all that had been done. And it was Chris who was going to pay.

And the key to it all was the last two pages of Charlie Zeff's novel, "A Songbird at Sundown", the pages which listed with pinpoint accuracy all the bombs Zeff had buried around the city over the years. And that list was his now. The last thing he had done before staggering into the hospital was buy a stamped envelope at the post office, enclose the critical two sheets of paper, and mail it to himself at his mother's house. Even now it was there waiting for him.

If Zeff hadn't given him the book to read back there in the trailer, or if he hadn't refused to hand it over when Holmes came out of the hole, Holmes knew that events may have taken a different turn. Yet it was Zeff's refusal to divulge the location of the variable signal transmitter that had driven Holmes into a frenzy of rage. Zeff had said he had such a device, hand-built from components bought at Radio Shack, and Holmes, who initially had given Zeff a severe beating in order to obtain the carefully typed list he wanted, now threatened to cut the writer's throat unless he forked over the small, battery-powered unit. In the end, Zeff, bloodied and weeping, had pointed to the oven. Holmes found the transmitter inside a cast iron pot. Grabbing a short, stiff-bladed knife, he stuck it deep in the little man's throat and sliced upward savagely. Crimson foam bubbled from Charlie Zeff's throat and, gurgling, his left leg kicking convulsively, he fell across the wildly scattered pages of his sad, dramatic manuscripts and died there on the faded linoleum in the kitchen of the old farmhouse.

* * *

Nancy had started carrying a gun. It was a chrome-plated .25 cal. Smith & Wesson. She had also begun to spend a lot of time reading the bible. One afternoon, out of the blue, she said to me: "Chris, have you ever considered the possibility that we might have this whole life and death thing figured backwards!"

I asked her what she meant.

"I mean just what I said, that we might have it backwards. No human being is a native of this earth; we're all just visitors, travelers, sojourners. When we're born we leave our home and come to this place for a little while and when we die we go back to our real home. So instead of fighting tooth and nail to stay alive here on earth for as long as we can, maybe we should admit we are strangers in a strange land and let ourselves ache a bit for the day we can go back where we came from."

"I've thought of that a hundred times, Nancy, but self-survival has to be an essential part of every living creature or no one would eat, fight, or hide from the wind. All life would cease to be."

Nancy was lying on the couch. She was in a dreamy mood. "I've just been reading John 14," she said, "and it's very comforting. Yes, Chris, I think we might have it back-wards. We should weep with sorrow whenever a new baby is born into this vale of tears and we should sing with joy whenever anybody dies. Because the dead are home at last. For them there is no more loneliness, no more hail-storms, no more sickness or pain or sorrow."

"And no more rapists," I said bleakly.

"That's right! So I'm going to start concentrating on where I'm going instead of worrying about where I am. They say that at the instant of birth all memory of who we are or where we came from is cancelled from our brain. It's called the Veil of Forgetfulness. I can see why this has to be. It simply wouldn't be fair to other people if some of us could think back and remember. But even if I can't pierce that veil I'm going to focus on what's behind it and to hell with this world and everybody in it."

Nancy shut her eyes. She was silent so long that I thought she'd fallen asleep. But she hadn't. "Chris," she said softly, "do you remember that sonnet I wrote for English class at St. Anthony's? I called it 'Sonnet Two'." She began to recite it:

"That stuffed toy panda treasured long ago,
Outlived itself; became too limp and gray,
Then left a tearful child prepared to know
A greater grief when puppies ran away.
The laughing children scattered as they grew
And farewell shouts broke ties we thought were fast;
Time saw us wave to more than just a few
Well-cherished dreams we'd hoped would always last.
When hunger left the starving lips that kissed
And innocence departed in the night,
What was there in the place of all we missed
But deep conviction those once scorned were right
Who said man's life from birth until he dies
Is one long sweet sad series of goodbyes."

*

"I always thought that was a very sad poem," I said to Nancy.

"It's not sad at all," she replied; "it's just metrical reality. But when I wrote it, it was from the point of view of someone standing in one spot waving goodbye to those that passed, moved away, or died. 'Goodbye' is only sad to people who either don't understand, or refuse to accept, what we were just talking about: that this is not our real home.

"The sonnet still applies, Chris," she went on, "only now I'm not saying goodbye to them, I'm saying goodbye from me--which is not at all the same thing. In other words, you and I both are about ready soon to depart, Chris: don't you agree?"

"Then why did you buy the gun, Nancy!"

"I bought the gun because as long as I'm here I'm going to play the game right up to when the final whistle blows. Just because I believe in eternity doesn't mean I'm going to let some weirdo punch me around; no way, baby!"

"Are you worried about Holmes?"

Nancy laughed. "No. As a matter of fact he's my number one source of satisfaction. He's my raison d'etre! The thought of that eunuch running around town, totally neutralized, makes me feel better than if he were sitting in the electric chair. Chris, dammit! this is the only way to handle rapos. I'll bet you if you took a poll that the vast majority of all taxpayers would agree with me. A little jail time, sure, that's great! but first and foremost a trip to the surgeon! And as far as breaching anyone's civil rights goes, I say shit on that. When all is said and done there is something to be said for the vigilante approach. Let's face it, a group who takes the law into their own hands might make a mistake. But when it's the victim who responds there can be no mistake. So I'm a vigilante and I'm a damn good one and I'm proud of it. And if there were more women like me there'd be a lot fewer rapos."

"There's a new crop coming every year," I reminded her.

"Ah, but wouldn't we thin the ranks of the repeaters!" Nancy got up from the couch now and put her Douay-Reims bible back on the shelf. "But anyway, Chris, you'll have to agree that you and me both are getting close to curtain call."

"You're right," I said.

"And isn't it grand! No more starting all over for me, Chris; no more back to Square One. And no more living in old rooms. Every time I move into a new place I remind myself that someone else just abandoned it. No matter how much I like it I can hear them saying: 'Thank God I'm finally getting out of this dump'! It's liking dating a divorced man. Heck, yeah! I'm sick of it, I tell you. I've done it all--and so have you. Everything from this point on is merely repetition." Nancy went into the bathroom and shut the door.

"How come you're talking so much today," I called out to her.

"Let not your heart be troubled," she shouted back; "behold! I am with thee."

I sat there awhile, smiling and thinking. I had really enjoyed this chat with Nancy, even though she had done all the talking. It was a comfort to clearly understand that to die was merely to go home. I had always known this, of course, yet hearing it said at this particular time filled me with a sense of relief.

* * *

At his ordination, in 1956, Russell Talbot prostrated himself before God and his bishop and took perpetual vows of poverty, chastity, and obedience. These days he lived with his wife Madeline and their three teenage children in a well-appointed condominium overlooking Lake Calhoun.

He was a short, rather muscular man of about fifty. It was the middle of the afternoon when Eckman and I arrived at his home. He took us out on the patio and poured us each a Coke. "So you liked my lecture at St. Joan of Arc," he said, leaning back in a brightly-webbed chaise-longue and smiling at us. "I find that rather fascinating because it happens that I have never spoken at that particular church. Now tell me, what is it really that brings you here?"

"We wanted to talk to an ex-priest," I said bluntly; "we wanted to ask a few questions."

He shrugged. "Fire away."

Eckman rattled the ice-cubes in his empty glass. "Do you have any whisky, Father?"

"I do," was the reply, "but I wonder if maybe you haven't had enough."

The man was right. Eckman had been drinking for three days and it showed. At first I had not wanted him to come along with me but then I figured, what the hell, I'm not trying to win friends and influence people. So I didn't argue about the matter.

"Do you know anything about us?" I asked Talbot.

"Certainly I do. That's why I invited you over here when you phoned. I have a great curiosity about people like you. I've seen you both on television and I've read about you in the newspapers so, yes, you could say I know a bit about you."

"How do you like our little cabal," I asked.

"I consider it an interesting product of the times," he said. It's fascinating that as the world becomes more troubled people develop an increasing need to join some group, any group. Apparently, belonging to something reduces their anxiety and makes life a bit more bearable."

"You're hardly the exception," I said. "Aren't you the head of that Alliance of North American Priests?"

Either he didn't hear me or he chose not to answer. "I have a friend in the bowling supply business," he went on, "and this fellow sells an absolutely unbelievable number of polyester warm-up jackets every year. These jackets have the name of a team, or an establishment, on the back and the demand for them is simply enormous. And it isn't just bowling teams that buy them either; he sells them by the tens of thousands to bars, taverns, pool halls, seed companies, schools, even churches. As a single mass culture rises to dominate America it seems there are fewer and fewer people willing--or able--to function as individualists."

Eckman made it clear he wasn't interested. "Why did you quit the Catholic church," he asked bluntly.

If Talbot was annoyed he gave no sign of it. "To the contrary, I happen to be very active in the church."

"But you're not a priest," I said.

"Certainly I'm a priest," he replied. "I'll always be a priest."

"Priests don't fuck," Eckman said,

chucking his ice-cubes over the balcony railing.

Talbot was silent for a moment. He looked off in the distance and appeared to be making up his mind about something. "I was dispensed from my vows," he said finally. "I went through the ecclesiastical court in Rome; a three-year process, I might add."

"All very kosher, eh," Eckman said.

"Quite!"

Now Talbot looked at me closely. "Maybe it's my turn to ask a question now," he said. "Tell me, where do you people get the kind of money you throw around?"

"What money?" I asked.

He gestured down toward my 450 SL parked at the curb eight stories below. "That car, for example."

I was annoyed to realize he must have been watching our arrival. "Yes, that's my car. Other people drive it more than I do but it's my car."

"Why the California plates?" he asked.

Had he been watching with binoculars? "Because I happened to be living out there when I got it," I snapped; "what of it!"

"You still haven't answered my question," he said, "but be that as it may. I'm still trying to figure out why you're here. What do you want?"

"We want you to give us a drink," Eckman said, standing up. "Come on, Chris, let's make it. Talking to this jack-off is boring as hell."

Quick as a cat Talbot was on his feet and standing next to Eckman. "What was that you just called me," he said pleasantly.

Eckman faced the smaller man squarely. "A jack-off and a two-bit turd," he said.

"Would you care to retract that and apologize or would you prefer to get the piss slapped out of you!"

Eckman started to smile. "By who? You? Listen, old man, show me a priest who dropped out of the church and got married and I'll show you a guy too horny to keep his pants zippered up!"

In the blink of an eye Talbot hit Eckman with two left jabs to the heart and a blurring right cross that tumbled Eckman to his knees. Then, chuckling, he walked into the house and came back a moment later with a liter of Canadian Club. "Your friend here should learn to watch his mouth before it gets him in serious trouble," he said to me.

"Fast hands," I muttered.

He heard me. "Oh, yes! I was Golden Gloves Champion in 1951; runner-up in Chicago on a TKO. It's like typing; your hands never forget!"

Eckman, groggy, got himself up on a chair. Talbot poured some C.C. in a glass and took it over to him. "Here, Mr. Eckman, drink this. You'll be all right. I didn't hurt you. I could have fractured your skull if I wanted to but I think you have problems enough."

Eckman took the drink and said nothing.

"We've got to be running along," I said, "but first I want to say something."

"Sure, go ahead. I'm still wondering what's on your mind. You've been here twenty minutes and haven't said anything yet."

I let him have it. "How can a person with your intelligence even pretend to believe in the teachings of a church that has betrayed as many people as has the Roman Catholic Church. Don't answer me now but I'm asking if you yourself would ever be so cruel to your children as to introduce them to this phony-ass bunch of baloney and take advantage of their trust in you by telling them that any part of it was anything more than a masterfully plotted scheme devised by clever men for their own devious purposes.

"Christ in heaven, Talbot, just think of what we were taught in school—and you're not that much older than I am, so you and I came out of the same generation and you know I'm telling the truth. The Baltimore Catechism; remember how we had to memorize every question and every answer! Oh, yes! And if we had any food or water after midnight when we were planning to go to communion it was a mortal sin. So was eating meat on Friday, or missing Mass on Sunday, or going to a "C" movie on the Legion of Decency. A mortal sin, buddy, and you know what that means. You die with one of those babies on your soul and you're going to burn in hell for all eternity. Not just for ten million years, dammit, but forever!

"And sex . . . my God, don't you dare ever mention that dirty, filthy word . . . don't you even *think* about it . . . or Satan will grab you for sure! And how about all the other lies we had crammed down our throats. Like the Latin Mass was forever, like only a priest can forgive sins, like divorced people could never remarry, like "Thou are a priest forever', like fallen-away Catholics are all sinners,--and on and on and on.

"Did you ever read any of Hitler's speeches, Talbot? I have. And, I swear to God, whole sections of them are lifted word for word from the teachings of the Catholic church. 'The primary function of marriage is the procreation of children'. That's Hitler talking, man, and I'll give you one guess where he learned it. Who knows how the world would have turned out if Hitler hadn't been born and reared a Catholic. Because whatever else he was he certainly was a master of power politics and anyone who wants to excel in this area would do well to sit down and study Roman Catholicism--as he did--because these cats in Rome really know how to do it. They have human nature figured out--all the wants

and needs and fears—and they use this knowledge to exploit people for the benefit of
themselves, the Church. The individual means
nothing; it's the group that counts. Shit! it's
only good sense to forbid people to divorce.
No matter how savagely a woman is beaten or
starved or neglected or abused; threaten her
with the fire of hell if she leaves her husband.
Force her to hang in there and you might get
one more baby out of her, or two, or ten.
Because to any ambitious cult, babies are the
most important thing in the world. Once you
get the babies you're safe for another generation. Everybody knows that; Rome, Hitler,
even the Mafia . . .

    "And so it's over at last, Talbot. The
bubble has finally burst. What all the persecu-
tion of two thousand years could not accom-
plish was done with a stroke of the pen by
Pope John 23. We were all betrayed. You and
me and all those millions of people who went
before us. Can't you just see them trudging
through the snow mile after mile, year after
year, trying to make it to Sunday Mass. Can't
you picture them lighting votive candles and
making the stations of the cross and teaching
their kids about limbo, St. Christopher, and
The Little Flower! And to think that it was all
just a cruel joke!

    "I remember talking to this behavioral
scientist once and he said to me: 'We've made
an exhaustive study of the criminal mentality

and that's one of many traits that you people have in common: you took the religious training of your childhood literally.' I said to this guy: "You bet your ass I took it literally; why? wasn't I supposed to?'

"So there you are. I was a sucker once, my man, but I won't be a sucker twice!"

"Do you want me to say anything," Talbot asked.

"You've already said it all," I told him. You've said it with your actions. When you broke the vows you made on your ordination day you told the world what you think of the Roman Catholic Church. You also defined your priorities and in doing so you told the world everything they could ever possibly want to know about you."

Talbot stood up. "If that's all you have to say then perhaps you will excuse me. I have work to do. And I might add that I expected something better from you." He looked glum.

"Let's go, Eckman," I said; "we've got work to do too." Eckman had been sitting there quietly while I gave Talbot my little speech. He stood up now and all three of us walked through the living room toward the door. "There is one last thing I'd like to ask," I said. "Would you consider going to confession, donning the vestments, and rejoining your church as a humble, repentant priest?"

Talbot opened the door and gestured toward the hallway. "Please," he said. "Go."

"Thanks for the whisky," Eckman said, "and here is my parting thought. If a guy like you can get dispensed from his vows in an ecclesiastical court, then why is it that a married Catholic can't get dispensed from marriage vows in that same court! And since you didn't care enough about your first three vows to bother keeping them, then what kind of a person would ever believe you when you took a fourth vow; like when you got married, for example!"

Talbot's voice was cold as ice. "You were leaving?"

We were and we did.

* * *

Holmes set off the first two bombs in Minneapolis on the Friday before Memorial Day. One was in the restroom of a large department store and the other in a parking ramp. The explosions came forty minutes apart, shortly before noon.

In the restroom he had entered the third cubicle from the back and, following Zeff's diagram, had turned the two dials to the correct frequency, pressed the short, stainless steel prong of the transmitter firmly to the green tiles in the floor, and turned on the switch for ten seconds. Then he switched it off and, leaving hurriedly, he was out of the store and back on the street when the explosion came. Even at this distance Holmes clearly felt the shock travel from the sidewalk through the soles of his shoes and the big plate-glass windows trembled visibly. He found it hard to believe that the small, unimpressive looking transmitter could do such damage. Hardly larger than a camera, powered by four nine-volt batteries, it weighed no more than two pounds. But it worked. Silently and efficiently it did its deadly job.

Holmes walked directly to the parking ramp. Here he consulted his list for the necessary frequency then pressed the probe into the base of one of the thick support columns and threw the switch. This time he was nearly to Hennepin Avenue before the blast came, shaking the loop and tumbling several parked cars and a truck off the top level of the ramp down onto the street sixty feet below.

Holmes, the transmitter in a plain brown bag, bought a ticket at a movie theatre and found a seat in one of the nearly deserted back rows. Outside, the sound of many sirens filled the air as people scurried this way and that in the confusion and excitement of the blasts. This would be a good place to organize his thoughts. It was cool and dark and safe and he had things to think about.

Like a poisonous vine, the anguish of his empty loins had spread to fill every bone and fiber of Holmes' body. His heart and chest were filled by the dull ache and every tomorrow had congealed into a blank gray wall through which neither hope nor life could be seen.

What was that faint vague stirring in the deep recesses. Was it a shadow of shame? Was he the final wasted shell of the boy who once had shone so brightly at track meets, on the diamond, and in the ring? What happened to the dream of someday competing in the Olympics! How had this nightmare started and when did it end.

Two bombs down; a hundred and fifteen to go! One by one he would set them all off. Let the honkys scramble. Did anybody die today? If not they will sooner or later. Lots of them! Eventually he would let the pigs know that he'd quit it if they'd give Chris to him. No, that wouldn't work. He'd have to get Chris himself. But how?

When had Bubba said the big C.O.B.R.A. gathering was set for . . . Sunday? Yes, sundown Sunday; Loring Park. Well, now . . . maybe the way to do it was to slip around and let a few of the brothers know that he was the one with the list of bombs. Hot damn! that was it! He'd spread the word that they could have the list in exchange for Chris. Oh, wouldn't they freak out to get that list! They could raise some pure, holy shit! Money, ransom, banks, cars, no kind of a demand was too far out once these crazy bastards had those hundred and fifteen bombs to work with. And no need to hand over the entire list. Hell! he'd give 'em fifty locations and tell them that's all there were; the rest he'd keep for a rainy day.

But, no . . . every day was a rainy day now. For him there was no future; for Roosevelt Holmes it was all over. Besides, there was only one transmitter. No, they could have the whole list. All he wanted was Chris.

And Savanna too. That was the phony muther who had sucked him into this whole mess. Yes, Savanna had to be dealt with too-- once and for all. He could figure out the details later. There was no big rush. No one was looking for him.

Completely oblivious to the movie, Holmes leaned back in his seat, clutched his precious paper bag closely, and shut his eyes.

* * *

Cecil Cohen didn't go near the farm-house until several days after the Bureau of Criminal Apprehension people had left. He stayed in his trailer at the bottom of the hill and busied himself with small chores. He cut the weeds that had sprung up at the foot of the windmill, cleaned last year's nests from the birdhouses, and dragged some of the more unsightly pieces of fallen tree limbs to the brush pile by the pond. One of these days he would put a match to that pile.

The old farmhouse stood empty and forlorn now. Gray and weather-beaten it sagged east. Shingles were missing and many of the windows were cracked and broken. It looked like it was ready to collapse. When Cecil finally did walk up there and go in the kitchen he found there was nothing to do but sweep and mop the floor.

Poor old Charlie Zeff, he found himself thinking. Did he have any family? Where would he be buried? What had become of all his manuscripts? Maybe it had been a mistake to let Charlie move out here. Maybe none of this would have happened if . . . but, no, a person didn't want to ever try and undo the past. What was done was done. The moving finger writes and having writ, moves on, nor all your piety and wit, shall lure it back to cancel half a line, nor all your tears wash out one word of it. Cecil Cohen felt the tears well up in his eyes as he put away his mop and broom.

Yes, the time had definitely come to let the old place go. There was no point in hanging on here any longer, no point at all. He'd get hold of the people at the United Farm Agency and let them take care of it. How odd when we say we 'own' some land, he thought, leaving the farmhouse and walking back down the hill. No one 'owns' anything, not really. A title was nothing but a sort of understanding that other people would stay away from you for the few short years of your life. But 'own'? Not hardly. The same land he walked on now was here a million years ago, it was here two hundred years ago when the Indians roamed across it, and it would be here long after the footprints of Cecil Cohen had been erased in the dust.

So this was the last farewell. Maybe he'd take the train back to L.A. No hurry to get there. This time it was a one-way ride and he might as well take in some of the scenery along the way. The Rocky Mountains were lovely this time of year.

How strange to find it was so easy to cut the ties that bind. Who would ever think that he, Cecil Cohen, could pick up a pen and with one flourish sign away the land he had held and loved so long. But it was time to move along now; there was no need to linger anymore. This land had served him and Camille well. It had fed and clothed and sheltered them all their adult lives. More than that it had given them a sense of stability during the time when this need was strong. But those days were gone. Time now to turn over the reins.

It would be good to get back to Rick's Restaurant again, good to walk in the warm California rain, good to follow Jack Smith's adventures in the Times, and good to hear the mockingbird.

He'd stop in at City Hall and tell the detectives he was heading back for the coast. If they came up with something they wanted to talk to him about they could write or phone. They knew his address and they knew his phone number.

That afternoon, a suitcase in each hand, he started hiking the two miles into town. The Greyhound didn't go through until 4:20; there was no hurry. Cecil was glad he had cleaned out all the birdhouses and he noticed with pleasure that the new corn was already three inches tall. "God's in his heaven," he said softly . . .

* * *

Even now Donald Eckman found it hard to believe how ridiculously, idiotically simple it had all been. It was almost as though another force, not he, had pulled the strings and made the moves. What little defense the world has, he thought, against a man who moves with certainty, strength, and with cold-blooded, mathematical precision. He was back in the old farmhouse kitchen now, marveling at what he had accomplished in the past twelve hours and sardonically reflecting on what certainly must come before this day was over.

Somewhere under the ground in the trailer or maybe lying with broken legs at the bottom of the entry shaft, were the three people who represented everything he despised in humanity. Skorpios, Russell Talbot, and Edna Moon, owner of a lesbian bar on Third Street. Abducting them, tying their hands tightly behind their back, and transporting them out here to the farm had been remarkably easy. Three hundred dollars cash to each of four black C.O.B.R.A. brothers had eliminated any need for him to so much as soil his hands in the process. All he'd had to do was drive the van up here with three cursing, pleading, begging, praying animals in back and, once here, drag them one by one, kicking and fighting, over to the open shaft and boot them down the hole. Whether they died in the fall, or got into the trailer, or only lay in a heap at the bottom, Eckman neither knew nor cared.

When the last of the three, Talbot, had been pitched screaming into the hole, Eckman rolled a fifty-gallon drum of No. 1 fuel over to the opening, uncapped it, and let the full barrel slosh down the hole. Later, after the police got here, and he'd had his fun with them, he would ignite that oil and the last sound he hoped he heard on this earth was the screams of those three maggots as they burned alive deep in the guts of the ground.

That the police would eventually get here was a foregone conclusion. There had been plenty of eyewitnesses when all three people had been grabbed and, although the four black men had been masked, the van used was the same one parked now in plain sight in the driveway. Simply getting here without being apprehended was a minor miracle in itself, especially considering that he had driven out the most direct route, heavily travelled Highway 12.

"Come on, fellows," Eckman heard himself saying, peering out a window toward the road; "let's get on with the show." He decided that if they weren't here in twenty more minutes he would set fire to the barn. That was bound to attract attention--and no matter who came first, fireman, police, or neighbors, the mines he would set off would bring more people, and more, until he had them here thick as ants at a jelly sandwich in the grass. And then, by God, he'd give them something they'd never forget. Yes, sir, these clowns didn't know it but they were in for a knock-down, drag-out picnic that would hit the front pages of every paper in the world. For himself there was one exit only but this was definitely known as Going Out in Style and Eckman looked forward to what was coming with eagerness and impatience.

Once again he checked the control panel Zeff had built and installed in the root cellar. Altogether it had thirty-two sets of wires leading into it, each set soldered to a switch and each connected to an ammonium nitrate or a plastique mine buried somewhere on the grounds. One bomb was buried at the main entrance, another two in the ditch, half a dozen behind various trees, two by the woodpile, two behind where the van was parked, one at both the front and side door of the house, three in the driveway itself, one by the chicken coop, one behind the granary, two behind Cecil's trailer . . . in fact, in every place that men besieging the house would be likely to crouch for cover there was one or more bombs buried, each with its own set of wires leading to Eckman's control panel. The jelly sandwich was lying in the grass; very shortly now the swarm of ants would appear.

In the time remaining there were a few last things to think about. Should he leave a note telling the cops it was Nancy who chopped up Holmes? But why! Just to save Chris? Why did he like Chris so much, he wondered. Because she is the absolute, number one, nerviest human being I ever met, he decided. God! I wish I could be like that . . . instead of working in a goddamn pet store!

A sudden spasm of coughing doubled up Eckman and he bent foreward sharply, resting his head on his knees and spitting up blobs of bloody gray sponge. Still the pain persisted and he rolled onto the floor clutching his elbows and trying to hold his breath to make the pain go away. I should have nailed me a cigarette manufacturer, he thought; that's who belongs in that hole. Jesus! what kind of a human being would make and sell cigarettes and inflict this on his fellow man! The pain eased off now and Eckman found himself musing on the days to come.

Chris herself won't live much longer, he decided. She's beaten the odds too many times and one of these days her luck is going to run out. But there'll be another Chris, and another, and still another, and somewhere along the line the world was going to have to figure out how to identify and deal with these people. The old stereotype of the criminal as an unshaven, ignorant, drunken bum who talked dese-dem-dose out of the side of the mouth was going to have to be put to rest. There was a whole new breed of cats out there that had to be dealt with. Truly brilliant people with big money connections, know-how, computers, and a total, complete lack of even the most basic precepts of morality. People ten thousand times more dangerous than the pitiful social misfits of the past, the mere John Dillingers, the Willie Suttons, the ridiculous Bonnie and Clydes. Did society really have any chance against this new breed? Eckman doubted it. How odd, he thought, that as America sinks deeper and deeper into the morass of its own immorality, the displays of self-rightousness are trumpeted louder and more frequently. As the number of abortions surpasses record levels, every fornicator in show biz lines up with some noble group. As

I.U.D. devices sell by the millions, toy safety becomes a major issue. As Penthouse sales soar, so do Save the Whales bumper stickers. America; land with a guilty conscience!

Eckman got up off the floor with a small groan. Wasn't there a pint of vodka in the cupboard? There was. Gratefully, he unscrewed the cap and let the wet fire roll down into his belly. "Here's to E.R.A.," he shouted gleefully, "and I hope you bitches get to someday live with it."

At that moment he heard a car coming down the road toward the house. Moving quickly to a window he pushed the curtain aside and glanced out. It was a tan and white sheriff's patrol. In a matter of seconds Eckman was in the root cellar scanning the carefully-labeled row of switches. Selecting switch #21, he flicked it on and ran back up the steps to watch. All the road mines were triggered by contact plates under the gravel. An instant after Eckman reached the window, with an enormous explosion, the squad car flew ten feet into the air, its hood and one wheel went flying, and it landed on its side in a tangle of crumpled steel and shattered glass while a cloud of dust and black smoke rose in the air.

Eckman laughed out loud. "One down! Come on, boys; come and get me. Let's have a little action around this fucking place!"

They came. In droves. The radio and

TV people came too. And Donald J. Eckman, coughing, spitting blood, and howling with vengeful glee, played out his role in the last sad drama of his life.

* * *

It was late in the day now. In less than an hour the sun would set. I had showered and dressed and I was glad I had washed and set my hair. It seemed appropriate that I looked nice, or at least felt that I looked nice, for this last C.O.B.R.A. meeting. In half an hour I would shut the door on this apartment and walk down to the park. Surely there would be an enormous turnout. Some would come from curiosity, some for the pot and beer, some to check on rumors they'd heard about Holmes, and some merely to kill time over the long holiday weekend.

For myself, I found I was filled with a moody emptiness of heart such as I never quite felt before. I lay down on my bed carefully, trying not to wrinkle my new red pantsuit, and, shutting my eyes, let the years and tears drift by. All the miles I'd travelled were done now. And all the heartbeats too. Through the fog of memory I found myself focusing for some reason on Arizona. How many decades had passed since I'd lived there in the Dragoon Mountains. How near they were again, and I heard myself murmuring, almost as a benediction: To Arizona.

Long years and miles away I lie awake,
When night has thrown her hush across the sky,
And sweetly does a distant music take
Me back again to precious days gone by.
I hear night winds that whispered long ago
Mix with the cries of coyotes that are gone,
While sputters from old campfires burning low,
Blend with a birdsong from a vanished dawn.
Elated now I'm lifted over grief,
To cast behind the shadow of despair,
But having learned such bouyancy is brief,
There comes again my melancholy prayer
That when the symphony shall fade away,
Its echo may survive the coming day.

* * *

Softly now, as gently as though moved
by angels, the curtain parted and clearly, in
perfect focus, I saw and I heard. Yet even
seeing and hearing I would not or could not
weep. For it was all so logical and predictable
and inevitable.

The park was jammed to overflowing
with the largest crowd I had ever seen. I
walked around slowly, mesmerized by the
sound and the fury. Shouts and howls of inane
laughter, transistor radios blaring, motorcycles
revved to an insane shriek, police car p.a. units
barking orders, bells, whistles, amplification

equipment producing painfully shrill arrows of feedback; it was Satan unloosed in the loop.

Dressed as I was, and with my hair down and shades to boot, no one recognized me. Even as I approached this insane asylum I knew I had no intention of mounting that stage to speak. No one could speak to these animals. They were too far gone. They had reverted to the cave and the club.

A dozen transistor radios were tuned to the station broadcasting live from Cecil Cohen's farm. Word of the carnage Eckman was creating spread rapidly through the park and soon fifty more radios picked it up, then two hundred more, and within minutes everyone was listening to the madly excited announcer. "Ladies and gentlemen," he was shouting, "I tell you, this is truly one of the greatest dramas of our time; the most terrible thing which has ever happened in our beautiful state. Three more police have just been killed in a stupendous explosion here, bring the total dead to, I believe, eighteen. Yes, eighteen brave policemen dead so far and no end in sight. Oh, pray God these mad dogs are flushed out soon, ladies and gentlemen . . ."

Every few minutes another explosion could be heard on the mass of radios in the park and at each one the crowd let out a great roar of approval.

"Folks, two additional highway troopers have just been reported severely wounded.

And word is spreading now that the governor may call in the National Guard very shortly if these barricaded killers cannot be brought down or somehow stopped. Tear gas bombs have been lobbed into the house but apparently the people inside have masks. Now there is a great tower of flame shooting into the air from over by the woodpile. Someone is screaming terribly. Oh! would you look at those flames leaping up! I'd say a gas line must have been ruptured. There is no indication of who is screaming. It sounds like more than one person! Oh, what terrible agony they must be in . . ."

Suddenly, not forty feet away, I saw Nancy in her new white dress. She looked like she was trying to get to the stage.

"Nancy," I screamed, but in all the confusion and noise she didn't hear me. Flailing my arms and using my elbows I fought my way toward her. And then, out of the mob of writhing people, two young policemen materialized and I saw them grab Nancy. I stumbled and fell to my knees. Clawing my way back on my feet I found a hole in the crowd and I was no more than six feet away when I saw that Nancy had somehow gotten free. The next thing I saw was the gun in her hand. Four shots rang out and both policemen staggered and fell, one of them spouting blood from a hole in his throat.

"Let's get out of here, Nance," I

screamed, grabbing her arm. The crowd opened before us and somehow we made it to the street. A line of empty squad cars was parked on Willow, their lights flashing and their motors running. Without a moment of hesitation I pushed Nancy into one of them, got behind the wheel, and burned rubber for eighty feet as I headed for the Black Dog plant. Enroute I triggered all my rooftop endless-loop transmitters and almost at once the gibberish began squawking from our radio.

At Black Dog, wasting no time, I retrieved the rifle I had hidden in a culvert and shot holes in all fifteen of the oil-cooled transformers. Then, siren on and red lights revolving, I floorboarded the big police cruiser and Nancy and I, at 130 MPH, flew straight down the Beltline for the waterworks.

But of course they had picked up our trail.

* * *

The waterworks was a madhouse of furious activity. At least twenty squad cars were racing around looking for Nancy. Carloads of C.O.B.R.A. people arrived and dumped out howling people who immediately attacked the police with bricks, stones, and an infinite variety of knives and handguns. Sirens and flashing red lights pierced the night and clouds of dust and smoke arose. Everywhere there were screams and shouts as gunfire mixed with cries and calls for help in a scene of total confusion and complete insanity.

There were at least five choppers overhead barking orders and sweeping the ground with their spotlights, adding their bit to the unbelievable chaos.

Across the river the city was dying in agony. Engulfed in darkness except for the lights of cars and fires, a gigantic cloud of smoke blanketed everything and yellow flames shot hundreds of feet in the air in thirty or more large fires. Windows cracked and fell from the towering IDS building and I could easily envision the hordes of looters, rapists, and murderers running amok in the streets while the police radios broadcast senseless gabble.

From time to time there was an enormous explosion as Holmes set off another of Zeff's bombs and even at this distance the screams of the tortured and the dying were clearly audible.

Nancy, in her white dress, had climbed a hundred feet up a high-voltage transmission tower. Where had she gotten the bullhorn? From a fallen cop?

"There she is," someone shouted; "on the tower."

"Shoot the crazy bitch!"

"Don't hurt her," I heard myself scream; "she's a victim of you sick bastards."

Almost at once a searchlight found her and locked on. Then another, and another, and now Nancy stood out brilliantly against the backdrop of the inky black sky. She aimed the powerful voice amplifier down at us and began to speak with great passion:

"And I heard another voice from heaven saying, Go out from her, my people, that you may not share in her sins, and that you may not receive of her plagues. For her sins have reached even to heaven, and the Lord has remembered her iniquities. Render to her as she also has rendered, and give her the double according to her works; in the cup that she has mixed, mix for her double. As much as she glorified herself and gave herself to wantoness, so much torment and mourning give to her. Because in her heart she says, 'I sit a queen, I am no widow, and I shall not see mourning'. Therefore in one day her plagues shall come, death and mourning and famine: and she shall be burnt up in fire; for strong is God who will judge her."

Three shots were fired, then more, and still more. The bullhorn fell from Nancy's hand but she clung there for a moment longer, high in the bright light above us.

I looked down at the little transmitter in my hand. It was black with a single pale-green button. From where I stood at least seven of my IVG-5 cannisters were within its range. Very slowly, using my left hand, I extended the telescoped antenna and then, looking up again, I saw Nancy dropping from the tower with the grace and beauty of a falling star. She hit the ground with a sickening thud and lay perfectly still in a grotesque little pile, parts of her white dress ruffling in the chill night wind. Unable to reach her side I stayed in the distance and, poignantly, recalled the last words Nancy had spoken to me before we had been separated.

"Do you have any regrets?" I had asked her.

"Yes," she replied, "I'm sorry I never learned to fish."

Now, in the demonic stink of a world gone mad, surrounded by maggots and banshees, I heard myself murmuring once again those awful words from long ago and far away. "Woe, woe, the great city, Babylon, the strong city, for in one hour has thy judgment come!"

And then, deliberately and firmly, I pushed the pale-green button.

* * *

January-May, 1980
The Breault Farm
Howard Lake, Minnesota

ABOUT THE AUTHOR

James Vincent Adams was born April 6, 1932, in Minneapolis Minnesota. His father was a highly successful traveling salesman who sold paper, school supplies, and firecrackers. His mother, an Irish orphan, was a piano player who died at age 32 from a cerebral hemorrhage, leaving two children: Mary, 3, and James, 16 months.

James and his sister then moved into the home of an aunt, "Vee" Donovan, where his father was the sole support of eleven people until 1935, when he remarried.

Busy with her own flock, which was eventually to number four, James' new stepmother granted almost total freedom to the boy and he was later to often state that he had never known an American child who was given such an opportunity to explore, discover, and learn.

He is three-fourths Irish, one-eighth German, and one-eighth Bohemian. His family, whose original name was Adamski, have been farming in the Southern Minnesota (New Richland) area for over 150 years.

Never a good student, Adams graduated from DeLaSalle High School, Minneapolis, in 1950, ranked 75 in a class of 141. When the Korean War broke out, he enlisted in the United States Air Force and was sent to Suwon, Korea. Although trained as a radar repairman, Adams later admitted he did little in Korea but sell whiskey on the black market.

In 1955 he was expelled from Marquette University, Milwaukee, for drinking on campus and, after a string of robberies, began serving a series of prison sentences which was to find him seven years behind bars before he was released on November 22, 1963.

In the years that followed, Adams lived a life which certainly ranks as one of the most colorful of contemporary American writers. He has had sixty-two different jobs. Today, he is usually found in one of the old mining camps of the West, in Ireland, or on Fremont Street in Las Vegas.

His first book, "All the Cake I Want," an autobiography covering the first ten years of his adult life, was transcribed into Braille by the Minnesota Society for the blind.

Never married, he continues to write.